DECISION
TIME

Earl Sewell

DECISION TIME

KIMANI
TRU
™

Recycling programs
for this product may
not exist in your area.

DECISION TIME

ISBN-13: 978-0-373-83172-2

www.KimaniTRU.com

Printed in U.S.A.

"Choose hope over fear and unity over division."

Barack Obama

acknowledgments

This is the fourth installment of the Keysha's Drama series and its popularity continues to amaze me. As always there are so many people to thank but first I want to thank you, the reader. Especially those of you who for one reason or another had gotten out of the habit of reading but decided to give this book a try. I truly hope you enjoy this work of fiction and it inspires you to backtrack and read the first three books.

A special thank-you goes to the Hillcrest High School Book Club members who've been reading the series and have waited patiently for this book. Those members are La'Mesha Abrams, Isis Adams, Tempest Alexander, Jasmine Baines, Jeniece Baines, Nicole Brewer, Lasaundra Burt, Ariel Campbell, Ramon Dantley, Douglas Davis, Lequela Goins, Jessica Harris, Alexis Hatch, Cierra Haymer, Osazomon Imarenezor, Dalis Jackson, Lauren James, Vincentia Jones, Camille Latham, Katherine Latimer, Kyle Leach, Latasha Lee, Brittany Letts, Tasia Little, Myah Manson, Tesa McCann, Joshua Nixon, Joy

Otabor, Jelinda Pace, Ashley Plump, Jordan Rogers, Kenya Sherrill, Ashley Stanford, Jessica Stanford, Shaniqua Stanford, Angel Stephenson, Capri Sykes-Chidress, Sakyra Thomas, Matavia Trotter, Bryndi Weatherspoon, Lisa Williams and Lanise Wimberly.

Thank you to my family, Annette and Candice for all of your love and support you've shown me.

A special thank-you goes out to Susan Boler and Linda Wilson for always encouraging me and providing me invaluable support.

Thank you editor Glenda Howard for all that you've done for my career over the years. You are truly one of a kind.

Please feel free to drop me a line at earl@earlsewell.com. Please put the title of my book in the subject line so that I know your message to me is not spam.

Make sure you check out www.earlsewell.com and www.myspace.com/earlsewell. Also visit the fictional character Keysha at www.myspace.com/keyshasdrama. You can also hit me up at www.keyshasdrama.ning.com. I'm also on Facebook and Twitter. Just type in my name and you should be able to find me with little difficulty.

one

KEYSHA

I swear my life should be turned into a movie or at a minimum a mini drama series. I just know one of the cable stations would leap at the chance to produce my life story. Over the past several months I've been dealing with more drama than any celebrity who has made tabloid headlines. Just when I think everything is settling down and some type of normality is taking shape, another major catastrophe explodes in my path and tosses my world back into a chaotic spin. I'm surprised I haven't completely lost my marbles yet because I certainly have enough stress.

I came up with a brilliant idea, like two seconds ago, to start keeping an electronic diary. I figure that if I can just express how I feel about all of the madness that's going on in my life, it would help. I once heard Tyra Banks say that writing can be therapeutic. I'm not saying that I'm crazy or need therapy, because I don't. I just heard that writing your thoughts can help you cope with a lot of crap. Right now I'm sitting at the desk in my bedroom waiting for my computer to boot up. I have on my pink pajama pants, matching Tweety Bird top and my hair is tied up. Behind me on the floor are my blue jeans with the image of Tinker Bell spray-painted on the right leg, my Tinker Bell top and gym shoes. My room is a total mess, but I don't feel like cleaning it up right now.

"I have no clue what to write or where to even start," I muttered aloud to myself as I placed the palm of my right hand against my cheek. As I thought about my troubles, I got emotional and felt tears welling up in my eyes. I just learned that the love of my life, my boyfriend, Wesley, had been shot. Tears began trickling down my cheeks and onto my keyboard. I took a few deep breaths before I stood and walked over to my dresser and pulled a few Kleenex tissues. I then got into bed, positioned myself on my stomach and let out the sadness. When there were no more tears left to shed, I gathered myself and went back to my computer and stared at the blank screen.

"This writing stuff is so lame," I whispered and then exhaled a sigh of frustration. The silence in the room was pierced when I heard my brother, Mike, thundering up the stairs. I quickly sprang to my feet and shut my bedroom door because I wasn't in the mood to talk to anyone right now. I just wanted to be alone. After locking my bedroom door, I walked back over to my computer, placed my fingers on the keyboard and began to type.

It's been almost a year since I left the group home for at-risk teens. I moved from the south side of Chicago to the suburbs with my father, Jordan. I actually didn't have a choice in the matter at the time. I ended up at the group home when my mom, Justine, got arrested and subsequently detained until her court date. My father and I had never met until the day he came to visit me at the group home in order to verify that I was actually his child. That was a real interesting day to say the least. Once he got over the shock and surprise that I was his daughter, we had to try and figure out how I'd fit into his family. At the time, his wife, Barbara, was suspicious of me and my younger half brother, Mike, hated my guts. I didn't care much for them, either, but I was trapped in a situation that I couldn't get out of.

Eventually we were able to work through our differences and all get along. And then I met Wesley, the best boyfriend a girl could ask for. He helped me through some major issues in my life, especially one that involved a backstabbing girl named Liz Lloyd, who I thought was my friend. Wesley has always been there for me and for that I'll always be grateful.

A few weeks ago, Wesley and his father moved from South Holland, Illinois, to Indianapolis, Indiana, to live with Wesley's grandmother after his father got injured in an electrical fire that destroyed their house. Wesley hated leaving me, and loathed his new neighborhood. He was constantly getting picked on by the local gang members because he was new to the area. Now my worst fears have come true.

At that moment I heard someone knock on my door. I saved my diary entry and closed the page before walking over to my bedroom door.

"Mike, I don't want to talk right now," I said loudly.

"It's me, Barbara. Open up." I glanced down at the rotating gold doorknob and saw that Barbara was already trying to enter my room. I reluctantly unlocked the door and let her in. Glumly, I walked back over to my desk and sat down.

"Are you okay?" I could tell she was concerned, but I didn't want her sympathy right now. I was still feeling resentful about her refusal to let me see Wesley.

"No, I'm not okay. Would you be okay if Jordan was lying in some hospital half a world away?" I gave her a sarcastic glare. Although it was ten o'clock, I noticed Barbara still had on blue jeans and a black, long-sleeved sweater top. She usually slipped into her loungewear around nine. Barbara let out a frustrated sigh and ran her hands through her silky black shoulder-length hair. She had recently grown out her chic cropped cut, and her new style looked good. I think she was going through a phase where she wanted to look hip and younger. Especially now since there was another female in the house. I think she quietly wanted to step up her game. She didn't look bad or anything, it's just something I've noticed about her lately. As she entered my room, she stared at my clothes on the floor.

"You need to come pick this stuff up and—"

"Ugh!" I grumbled as I picked up my belongings and hung them up.

"I understand how you feel, Keysha, but look at it from our point of view. Jordan and I have just been through a lot with you and Mike. I mean, you guys literally had us pulling out our hair when we heard the police had picked you two up. The crap that you and Mike put us through is the kind of stuff that gives people heart attacks." Barbara folded her arms across her chest and glared at me. I wondered when Barbara was going to let that go. She was still angry about the incident where Mike took Jordan's car without permission to see Toya, a hood chick who lived in my old neighborhood. Things wouldn't have been so bad if the car hadn't gotten stolen by some thugs, who took it to an illegal chop shop. Mike and I got caught up in a police sting when we tried to get the car back. We were hauled off to the precinct for questioning, and didn't get released until Barbara and Jordan picked us up.

"But this has nothing to do with me and Mike being in trouble. This is Wesley, the boy who saved my life. The boy who cleared my name, the boy who came to my rescue and took action when no one else would. The least I can do is be by his side during his time of need." I pleaded my case then stopped to blow my nose and wipe away my tears.

"I know it's tough, Keysha," Barbara said, now trying to console me, but it wasn't helping. "But right now is not a good time. I'm sure Wesley will be fine. He's a tough kid and I'm sure he'll pull through." It felt like Barbara was feeding me a line of bullcrap.

"How can you sit here and say that? You don't even know if he was shot in the head or the chest." My temper quickly flared up because I didn't like for one minute how she was trying to glaze over the situation.

"And neither do you, Keysha. And don't use that tone

of voice with me," Barbara snapped. "It won't do any good to jump to conclusions until we get all the details."

"Please, I'm begging you. I need to go see Wesley. I need to be with him. I love him. Don't you understand how badly my heart is hurting? Can't you see that I can't live without him?" I looked deeply into her eyes, hoping my pitiful look would melt her heart.

"The answer is still no. Allow Wesley and his family to work through this crisis. They're going through a traumatic experience and we should—"

"Whatever!" I interrupted Barbara. I didn't want to hear anything else she had to say.

"Keysha, this is the last time I'm going to tell you about that tone of voice. I'm not playing with you, little girl. Don't make me lose my temper." I gave Barbara a defiant glare, but said nothing more.

"You have to stay focused on your schoolwork. You can't take a bunch of days off in the middle of the semester to sit by his side, so just get that thought out of your head." Barbara crossed her arms. "Now in the meantime both you and Mike need to be thankful that Jordan and I were able to get you out of the mess you were in without it going on your record." Barbara raised her voice at me and that upset me even more than I already was.

"Where is Jordan at?" I raised my voice at her, completely dismissing what she'd just said to me. I thought I could probably win him over if I really tried.

"He's in his damn skin!" Barbara screeched. Her eyes reflected the stress and aggravation Mike and I had put her through.

"I know you don't think you're going to make Jordan feel guilty with your pitiful eyes and sob story. It doesn't work like that. You cannot lay a guilt trip on Jordan about this. I guarantee you that," Barbara said, pausing and awaiting my response. I didn't say anything because my rising anger had placed a vise on my voice.

"We'll pray for Wesley's speedy recovery and send him some flowers, but you are not going to see him. Plus Jordan and I have decided to ground both of you."

"Ground me for what? I didn't do anything." I snarled back at Barbara. I didn't see any justification for me being grounded.

"Keysha, you tried to help Mike cover up that fact that he'd—"

"I wasn't trying to cover up anything." I was about to say more, but I paused for a moment. "You know what. Just forget it. My life is so screwed up it isn't even funny. I just want to be left alone."

"Okay. Have it your way. I'll leave you alone for now, but you're still not going to see Wesley," Barbara said in a firm tone as she made her way out the door.

"That's what you think," I uttered to myself. "I've been taking care of myself and doing my own thing long before I got here. And right now I'm damn sure not going to allow you to control me and run my life. I'm going to go see Wesley one way or another." A few seconds after Barbara left I got up, closed my door and rested my back against it. I stood there working out a plan in my mind about how I was going to run away to be with Wesley.

two

WESLEY

I heard muffled voices all around me. My brain was in a fog and I felt as if my mind was stuck somewhere between sleep and reality. I wasn't exactly sure where I was or who was around me because I had a difficult time getting my eyes to open. I tried to raise my right arm to get the attention of whoever was in the room, but my limb was stiff and immobile. I raised my left arm and cleared away the sleep debris between the bridge of my nose and the corner of my eyes. That simple act felt unusually difficult and I knew I'd been sleeping for a very long time. I finally opened my eyes, but couldn't focus on anything. Everything was hazy, cloudy and indistinguishable. I became very nervous and feared that somehow I'd become blind and paralyzed. I immediately did a quick body check. I wiggled my toes, moved my left arm, then craned my neck from right to left. Feeling confident I wasn't powerless, I opened my mouth and attempted to speak. It was then I realized my tongue and throat were as dry as desert sand. I tried to say something, but it was too painful.

"Wesley?" I heard a voice call to me from what seemed like a great distance away. "Wesley, if you can hear me, squeeze my hand." I felt the warmth of my father's hand in my own.

"Wesley," he spoke again. "Squeeze my hand." It seemed to take every bit of strength I had to grip him. *What's going on?* I thought as I willed myself to focus on the blurry silhouette of my father.

"Are you awake?" I squeezed my dad's hand again to signal I was conscious.

"The nurse is about to give you some pain medicine," my dad said. *Pain medicine? I can't feel a thing as it is. Why do I need pain medicine?* I wondered.

Then without warning, I felt myself slipping away from reality and drifting back into a very deep sleep.

I opened my eyes again. This time I knew I was fully awake because I was able to focus on objects like the bed curtain, the nightstand and the telephone. I slowly craned my neck to the left and saw the blinds on the window were drawn shut. I glanced over to my right and saw my father slumped down in a chair. I attempted to say something, but my lips, tongue and throat were so devoid of natural moisture, I felt as if dry sand had been poured down my throat. I raised my head and glanced down at my body and tried to recall what happened to me. My right arm was in a sling and strapped to my body. My shoulder was burning, as if my skin was ablaze with searing heat. I reached up to touch my shoulder, but it was covered with a bandage. I glanced out the door and noticed a nurse wearing blue scrubs rushing past my bedroom door.

"I'm in a hospital," I mumbled as I tried to recall how I'd gotten there.

"Hey, champ. I see that you're awake now." My dad had risen to his feet and was now hovering above me. I tried to speak.

"No, no, no. Don't try to talk yet." Dad waved his hand as he tried to stop me from communicating, but I wouldn't. I needed water very badly. "Wesley." He caught my gaze and I tried as hard as I could to speak.

"Water," I strained my voice to say the word. My father held up his finger, which I interpreted as "wait a moment."

"Let me get something for you to write on." Dad stepped away and returned a brief period later with a pen and a pad.

"I know it's going to be difficult for you to write with your left hand, but write as best as you can." He placed the writing pad beneath my hand and gave me a pen to scribble with. I tried to write the letter W with my left hand, but it wasn't going so well.

"It's okay. Keep going. I think that's the letter U." My dad tried to decode my squiggle. I moved my hand back and forth vigorously across the page to scratch out the letter and tried writing again. When I was finished, my dad held up the piece of paper and tried to decipher my scrabbling.

"Let's see…that's a W and that's a T. I'm having a hard time making out the other letters, Wesley."

Come on, Dad, I thought to myself. *Work with me here. Don't get stupid on me now.*

"Wait a minute. I think that's the letter *A*." Dad paused in thought and then repeated the letters.

"*WTA.*" He looked at the page very perplexed as if he was trying to figure out a puzzle on *Wheel of Fortune*. "Water! You want some water, Wesley?" he asked.

I nodded my head. I almost wanted to say, "Duh!" But I didn't.

"Oh, no problem. I'll get some for you." He rushed out of the room, calling for the nurse. A short time later a doctor entered.

"Wesley, I'm Dr. Murphy, the surgeon who worked on you." Dr. Murphy appeared to be in his mid-fifties. He had a mixture of salt-and-pepper hair and eyelids that sloped downward, as if weather-beaten into saggy folds of skin by one too many hours of suntanning.

"I've asked your dad to sit outside in the waiting room with your grandmother while I examine your wound." *Wound?* I thought. *Jesus, what happened to me?*

"Now, Wesley, you may feel a burning or stinging sensation." I nodded as I braced myself for the pain.

"Okay, here we go."

"Aguuuh!" I tried to howl, but my voice couldn't produce the kind of painful moan I needed it to.

"You're one lucky guy, Wesley," Dr. Murphy explained as he continued examining me. I tried to speak again, but it hurt like hell.

"Don't talk just yet. I'll give you some water in a moment. When I do, you need to sip it—don't gulp because that's not going to feel good at all if you guzzle it." After he was done, a nurse came in and sat a plastic pitcher of water and cups by my nightstand. I was glad to see her. I did as the doctor suggested and sipped the water slowly. My first sip was like pouring water on cracked, dry soil.

"I'm going to go get your family. I'll be right back," Dr. Murphy said before exiting the room. I drank more water, which caused my stomach to grumble. I suddenly felt as if I was going to puke. I did my best to control the urge, but it wasn't easy.

Before long, Dr. Murphy returned with my dad and Grandmother Lorraine.

"Oh, I'm so happy to see you." My grandmother rushed over and kissed me on the forehead. Her lips felt like rose petals. I hugged her with my left arm and held on to her for a moment. When she finally pulled away, I noticed she was wearing a brown blouse with a matching headband. Grandmother Lorraine had blond dreadlocks that cascaded down her back. She was wearing her glasses, which had slid down to the tip of her nose. The brown freckles sprinkled beneath her eyes and on her cheeks stood out against her extremely light complexion.

"I was just telling Wesley just how lucky he is." Dr. Murphy stood beside my bed, placed his hands inside the pockets of his white lab coat and looked directly at me. "The bullet went straight through your shoulder. The projectile severed your clavicle bone and exited through your back. The bullet could've easily deviated and punctured a lung or broken a rib."

"I've been shot?" I asked for clarification.

"Yes, you have. It may take a little more time for everything to come back to you," explained Dr. Murphy.

"Certain types of trauma can cause a repression of short-term memory. You also suffered a concussion when your head slammed against the concrete. The force of the impact to the brain may cause blurred vision, vomiting and sometimes the loss of your short-term memory."

"He is going to remember everything, isn't he? Charges are going to have to be filed," my dad interrupted Dr. Murphy.

"It's hard to tell. Sometimes in cases like this a person can be told what occurred, but they can't remember the incident. In other cases, patients have temporary memory loss and experience flashbacks."

"Is this similar to what soldiers go through?" my dad asked.

"That's called post-traumatic stress disorder and happens when there is prolonged exposure to mental or emotional events. That's a little more severe. Overall, I believe that Wesley will recover physically and go on with his life. This particular episode may remain repressed or he could have full recall. Either way, I'll provide you with information to help him through that part of his recovery."

"Oh, thank You, Jesus," my grandmother blurted out as if a great anchor of uncertainty had been lifted from her heart.

"I had his name added to the prayer list at our church. There are a lot of good people pulling for him to make a full recovery," my grandmother said loudly and clasped her hands. "Praise God," she squealed. A smile crossed my face as I studied her. Everyone at my grandmother's church was familiar with her distinguished raspy voice. Nearly every Sunday she would do her fair share of shouting and testifying, yet it was still strong enough to command attention whenever she spoke. At that very moment there was a rapid succession of knocks at the door.

Two uniformed officers entered the room. "Hello, folks. I'm Officer Miles and this is my partner, Officer Davis. I was wondering if we could speak to Wesley for a moment. We need to ask him some questions."

"Sure. He just woke up not long ago and things are still a little fuzzy. He appears to be experiencing some memory loss," Dr. Murphy explained.

"Do you remember what happened?" asked my dad as he poured more water into my cup.

"I just can't concentrate right now," I whispered as I vainly tried to recall the incident.

"Can you tell me the last thing you remember?" asked Officer Miles as he pulled out a writing pad.

I shrugged my shoulders. "I just remember waking up in this room," I answered honestly.

"Do you remember what you were doing yesterday?" asked Officer Miles. I paused and tried to remember, but I got nothing.

"No," I answered as I continued to search my mind for answers or clues.

"We should talk to the girl," Officer Davis suggested to his partner. "If he can't remember, it's going to be difficult to get a conviction."

"Now hang on a minute. Don't give up on him. Give him a little more time to recover. He'll remember." My dad had gotten upset. "I don't want you guys to give up because of this."

"We'll talk to the girl and then we'll come back in a day or so to see if he can recall what took place," said Officer Davis.

"Well, I'm working on getting an attorney," my dad said.

"No need for you to do that right at this moment." Officer Miles removed a business card from his shirt pocket and handed it to my father. "Call this number and give them the police report number. They'll tell you which state prosecutor your case has been assigned to. We'll continue our investigation and provide them with a report of our findings." My dad exhaled loudly as he took the business card.

"Get well soon," said Officer Miles. He and Officer Davis turned and exited the room.

"I'll go and have the nurse order you some food," Dr. Murphy said before stepping out.

"Wesley, think back. What happened?" my dad pleaded.

"I don't know," I answered truthfully.

"That's it. Leave him alone," Grandmother Lorraine interrupted. "Let him get some rest." I picked up my cup of water and took a sip. Just as I finished off the cup, my mother walked into the room. Without acknowledging anyone, she moved past my father and grandmother and hugged me. She reeked of alcohol and cigarette smoke. After a short embrace she pulled away and glanced accusingly over at my father.

"Don't say a word to me and don't start saying a bunch of crap because I don't want to hear it," my dad snapped.

"I told you that Wesley was a handful, but at least when he lived with me he never ended up getting shot. Maybe I need to take you back to court and claim that you're an unfit father," my mother spat.

"Stop it! Both of you!" Grandmother Lorraine moved between them. "This is neither the time nor place for squabbling. Come on. Let's go out into the waiting room so Wesley can rest." Grandmother Lorraine escorted both of them out of my room. I then rested my head on the pillow, closed my eyes and groaned.

three

KEYSHA

I squeezed into my black one-piece bathing suit, then shoved my hair under the matching black swimming cap. My suit was a little tight-fitting. It seemed to have shrunk since the last time I wore it for swim class. I made a mental note to pick up a new one the next time I was at the mall. I could've rented a swimming suit, but something about a rented bathing suit just grossed me out. Once I got my bathing suit to completely cover my behind, I walked out of the locker room and onto the pool deck, shivering uncontrollably. I felt as if I'd just walked into a freezer. I immediately snatched up a large towel from a nearby rack and draped it over my shoulders to keep warm. The scent of the chlorine was extra strong, so I knew that by the end of the class my skin would be desert-dry and itchy, which meant that I'd be using a good amount of moisturizer. Another reason to hate my Monday-morning swim class.

"Hurry up, ladies, and take a seat on the bleachers," Miss McFadden, the swim teacher, bellowed out as she grabbed the attendance sheet for roll call.

"You know we're learning how to do the backstroke today," said Maya Carter just before I sat down next to her. Maya was my swimming partner and we were at the beginning stages of a friendship. I had met her not too long ago when our swim rotation in gym class began. The only reason that I said anything to her was because she seemed pretty cool. And she didn't hang with the snobby girls who were constantly gossiping about everybody.

"That is a very nice-looking tattoo," I said, admiring the details of the body art gracing her right shoulder.

"Thank you. My mom and dad still don't know that I ran off and got this yet. Believe it or not I've only had it for a few weeks. When my parents do find out they're going to hit the roof. Hopefully they won't find out until I'm like eighteen and grown." Maya laughed, but didn't seem overly concerned about keeping her secret away from her parents.

"Where did you get it done?" I asked out of curiosity. I'd never thought about getting a tattoo until that moment. I thought a rose or even perhaps getting something in memory of my deceased aunt Estelle would be worth looking into.

"I went to this tattoo parlor on Wilson Street. I can get the address and the name of the tattoo artist who did this for me if you'd like," Maya offered as she tucked her hair beneath her swimming cap.

Maya was part Latino, and part African-American. She

had a cute round face, brown eyes and recently arched eyebrows that made her eyes look mysterious. Pretty black hair cascaded down to her shoulders and she had a contagious laugh that made me want to smile and chuckle every time I heard it. She was an honor-roll student and a member of the drama club. It would have been easy to have been jealous of Maya. From my perspective, Maya seemed to have it all: beauty, brains and talent. She was even dating a hot guy named Misalo, who could dance just like Usher, or so I'd heard.

Maya was a junior like me and had two younger siblings, a sister named Anna, who was a freshman, and a brother named Cory, who was in seventh grade. Her mom worked for the state as a translator. Her mom spoke three languages—English, Spanish and Chinese. Her dad worked for ABC News in Chicago as a producer for the evening news. Maya didn't really know what she wanted to do with her life. Some days she wanted to be an actress, other days she wanted to be a therapist and sometimes she talked about being a talk show host. I personally believed that she'd make a good talk show host because she just loved to gab about everything. I don't know how her boyfriend, Misalo, puts up with her indecisiveness and her talkativeness. I mean, if I let her, Maya would talk my ear off.

"We're learning how to do the backstroke already? Dang, I just figured out how to do the dog paddle without splashing water in my face or sinking. Learning how to swim is such a struggle for me. Whenever I leave this class I'm completely exhausted." I was about to continue on with my whining, but Maya interrupted me and changed the subject.

"So how did your weekend at your mom's house go? I meant to call you, but I couldn't use my cell phone," Maya said as she yawned very loudly.

"How did you lose your phone?" I asked as I glanced down at my toes and wiggled them. I needed to give myself a pedicure because the red polish had started to chip on the second toe of my right foot.

"Girl, no. There is no way I'd ever lose my cell phone. You know I keep my cell phone attached to my ear, which is why the world seemed to have stopped spinning when my mom took it from me."

"Why did she take your cell phone away?" I asked, being nosier than usual.

"She blasted me for going over my minutes and texting too much. She got really ticked off when she got the cell phone bill. I mean, OMG, it's too hard trying to manage how many texts I send and receive. Although I will admit I sent Misalo so many messages that my thumb got sore. See." She held up her right thumb. "Kiss it. Make it feel better."

"Listen here, crazy girl, if you don't get your nasty thumb out of my face…" I warned as I shoved her hand away. "Your mom didn't go through your text messages, did she?" I asked, absolutely horrified at the thought of someone taking my phone and reading all of the texts that Wesley and I sent to each other. "I hope you didn't have any crazy or sexy conversations going on."

"No, I don't think that she did. Even if she had she would not have been able to unscramble what all the IM codes meant. She still doesn't know what BFF, LOL, or TTYL means. In fact, she thinks WTF means Wednesday,

Thursday and Friday. It's strange, she can speak all of those languages, but when it comes to texting, for some reason she is totally clueless. Seriously, though, how was your weekend with your real mom? Is she still trying to get you to do the scam thing?" That's another thing about Maya. The girl could talk about several subjects at one time and not miss a beat. How she's able to remember everything was a total mystery to me.

"Maya, all I have to say is that I had one hell of a weekend," I proclaimed, and threw my hands up.

"Really? Well come on, spill the beans and tell me what happened. I want all the details, too."

I glanced at Maya, who was on the edge of her seat with anticipation. It was clear that I had her full attention.

"Well?" she cajoled. "C'mon and spill the details."

Maya is a good person, but she's very nosy and the type of girl who could get you in trouble with a teacher for talking too much.

"Why do you care, Maya? I mean, honestly…you barely know me." I was a little suspicious and mistrustful of anyone who wanted to get close to me, especially after what I'd gone through with Liz Lloyd, a girl I met when I first attended the school. That friendship led me down a path of destruction where I was accused of selling drugs and caught a court case. I just didn't want to take any unnecessary chances.

"Well, I'll never get to know you if you don't talk. They don't teach Mind Reading 101 here." Maya laughed at her own joke. I laughed along with her, even though I really wasn't in a laughing mood.

"I'll give you the details about my horrific weekend some other time. I have a new dilemma I'm dealing with," I admitted just before I began to confide in her.

"What is it?" It was killing Maya not knowing. She was the type of person who'd hold up traffic so she could take in all the details of an accident until she was satisfied that she'd figured out what happened.

"I'm going to run away," I whispered.

"Run away!" Maya blurted. She didn't pick up on the fact that I was whispering.

"Shh, dang, girl, you've got a big mouth!" I scolded her for broadcasting our conversation to the world. "If you can't keep this between me and you, I'm not going to tell you a damn thing. In fact, I shouldn't be telling you at all because I don't think you can hold water."

"I'm sorry. I didn't mean to be so loud. It's just that that was the last thing I expected you to say. And for the record, I can keep a secret. I know plenty of stuff about a lot of people around here that I've never told anyone about." She paused for a moment and allowed me to digest what she'd just said. "What are you running away for?" she whispered.

"Wesley. I need to see him right way." We paused as Miss McFadden began to take attendance.

"I thought you said he was in Indianapolis," Maya said with a quizzical look on her face. "Here," she answered Miss McFadden just after she'd called out her name.

"He is, but I have to go to him. He needs me. I just know he does." My mind drifted away as I thought about Wesley and the turmoil he was undoubtedly going through.

"Keysha Kendall." Miss McFadden's voice broke through my thoughts.

"Here," I yelled.

"Keysha, you're not making any sense. What's the urgency? Did he get hit by a car or something?" Maya said jokingly.

"Yes," I answered in a tearful voice. "Wesley's been shot."

"Wesley got shot!" Maya once again announced to the entire gym class.

"Who has been shot?" Miss McFadden searched all of the faces in the bleachers for an answer. Then everyone turned and looked at Maya and me.

"No one," I immediately answered so that everyone would stop staring at us. As soon as Miss McFadden continued on with roll call I slapped Maya on the thigh. "I'm not telling you anything else if you're going to yell out like that," I growled through clenched teeth.

"I'm sorry. You just keep surprising me, that's all. I get a little excited sometimes. I don't mean anything by it." Maya was now whispering and being extra cautious about how she was reacting to what I was telling her.

"Where'd he get shot? Is he alive? Is he paralyzed? Why did you even come to school today?" Maya was firing off questions before I had a chance to answer them.

"All I know is that he's been shot and I need to get to him," I said, absolutely convinced of it.

"Well, can't you call the hospital at least to find out his condition?" Maya asked.

"I don't know what hospital he's in. I still have to find that out," I said, admitting that I knew very little.

"Then how are you going to go see him if you don't know where he is?" Maya glanced at me curiously.

"If his grandmother would just answer his phone so I can get some information from her, my life would be all the more simple. But I've been calling his cell phone nonstop and his crazy grandmother won't answer his damn phone. I mean, wow. Why wouldn't she answer his damn phone at a time like this?"

"Maybe she doesn't have his phone with her anymore," Maya suggested.

"That's bull. Even if she lost it, she should know how to get in touch with me. Whenever something tragic like this happens, people always stay in constant contact with their loved ones. I think she's ignoring my calls on purpose."

"Keysha, try to calm down," Maya said.

"I'm sorry, I'm just really wound up today," I admitted.

"I could use Google to find all of the hospitals in Indianapolis and then you could call each one of them and ask if Wesley is a patient," Maya said, offering her help.

"That's a great idea," I said, thinking that there couldn't be too many hospitals in Indianapolis. I suddenly felt confident that I'd find out exactly where he was.

"I have study hall after this. I'll use my time on the computer to start searching for you and then I'll text you the names and phone numbers of area hospitals," Maya said.

"But isn't your mom going to be upset if you get another high bill?" I asked.

"She'll just have to understand. This is literally life or death, right?" Maya asked, searching my eyes for confirmation that would justify her decision to help me.

"Yes, it is."

"Well then, it is what it is. That's just the kind of friend I am. I'm loyal, helpful and I tell it like it is. *And* I keep it real. I will go the extra mile for those who mean a lot to me," she said as she draped her arm around me. "Real friends like me are hard to come by, Keysha. I've got your back on this, girl. I'll help you any way that I can."

"You really don't have to do this, Maya, but I truly appreciate it. I may look calm on the outside, but on the inside I'm a nervous wreck." I admitted to the turmoil going on inside my heart.

"I would be, too. You just stay strong and we'll get through this together. Okay?" Maya smiled.

"Okay," I answered. Just then Miss McFadden blew her whistle and ordered us all to get in the pool.

"Come on," I said, grabbing Maya by the wrist and tugging her along behind me. "Hopefully the water won't be too cold today." I dreaded the fact that I had to focus on something other than Wesley.

four

WESLEY

I opened my eyes once again and my mind was much clearer than it had been earlier. I shifted my position on the lumpy hospital bed and glanced out the window. Nightfall had arrived. I rotated my head in the other direction and looked at the digital clock on the wall, which read 6:00 p.m. My father was asleep in the other patient bed. A black bible rested on his chest, which I knew belonged to my grandmother. She'd probably told him to pray for me. I laughed a little on the inside at the silliness of it, but then again, a sense of love and care blanketed me, knowing my father was the type of man who would get on his knees and pray. I was about to see how much mobility I had, but thought twice about making any sudden or dumb moves that would cause me pain or do further damage.

"Damn. Now I'll have to learn how to do everything with my left hand—brush my teeth, comb my hair, eat my food and even wipe my behind." I released a depressing sigh. I was in no way looking forward to the experience of teaching my left hand how to do all of the things my right hand did. I decided to lightly touch my shoulder where I'd been wounded. My shoulder felt numb. I attributed the lifelessness to the medication I was on.

A moment later, my thoughts drifted to my girlfriend, Keysha. Guilt plagued me and I knew she would be upset that I was in the hospital. She would be especially angry over the circumstances that landed me here. I didn't want to communicate that fact to her yet, and my grandmother Lorraine told me she would speak to Keysha. I vowed to call her once I was feeling stronger.

"Wow," I whispered softly. "How did my life get so far out of hand?" I closed my eyes for a moment and the name Lori popped into my mind.

"Why did I even get involved with her?" I asked myself as the memory of what had taken place began to come back to me.

Grandmother Lorraine's neighbor and good friend Miss Winston lived with her adult daughter and teenaged granddaughter, Lori. Lori was a junior just like me and attended the local high school I'd be going to until my house back in Illinois was renovated. Apparently, Grandmother Lorraine and Miss Winston thought it would be a good idea for Lori and I to meet. Then without any warning, Grandmother Lorraine invited the two of them over one afternoon. When they arrived, I was in my bedroom in the basement, chatting it up on the phone with

Keysha. My grandmother summoned me from the top of the staircase.

"Wesley, come up here," she called.

"I'm on the phone," I answered, irritated by the interruption of my conversation with Keysha.

"Boy, get off the phone and get your tail up here! When I call, you need to come running." Grandmother Lorraine was a little too old-school for me. She had this hang-up about respecting everything she said and honoring all of her requests, no matter how trivial they were. I reluctantly ended my phone call with Keysha and walked up the stairs to see why she was acting as if her hair was on fire.

"What do you want?" I asked, utterly frustrated. I figured Grandmother Lorraine was going to have me do some insignificant task like twist the lid off a jar or walk out to her car to retrieve an item she'd inadvertently left on the car seat. Ever since my dad and I arrived, I got the sense Grandmother Lorraine planned to use me as free labor. I couldn't wait for the contractors to finish rebuilding our home, which had been damaged from an electrical fire. It would be great to be back home, not worrying about stupid rules.

"Come on and follow me in here to the family room. I've invited some company over," she informed me. As I trailed behind her I marveled at how tall she was. Grandmother Lorraine stood no fewer than five feet ten inches. From what I understand of my family history, her father, a man named Bud, stood six feet six inches tall. He was a massive man who made a living as a bootlegger during the era of prohibition, when alcohol was illegal. From mythical stories I'd heard about Bud, he was the type of man who didn't take any mess off of anyone. Legend has it that his fuse was so short he once shot a man in the foot because he'd accidentally tripped up a set of stairs and broke several bottles of alcohol he was carrying for my great-grandfather. I believe Grandmother Lorraine inherited elements of Bud's no-nonsense personality. She was a feisty and bossy woman who could get on your nerves really quickly if you allowed her to get under your skin.

"I don't feel like meeting anyone," I huffed because I thought for sure she was about to parade me around in front of her elderly acquaintances.

"I didn't ask what you felt like doing." She stopped, turned toward me and snapped her fingers. "Now get that frown off of your face before I give you a left hook." I gave her a condescending look and thought, *Yeah right. You'll swing and miss, and I'll fall out of the floor laughing*. I gave her a sly grin when she turned, and I followed her into the living room, where the visitors were waiting. The living room was in need of a major overhaul. The sofa and love seat were red and white and covered with plastic. I swear, she must've gotten liquored up and gone out to a Valentine's Day door-buster furniture sale where she spent all of her cash. The furniture was old when my father was a teenager, which meant now it was ancient and needed to be donated to a museum. It was amazing that after all the years that had come to pass, the furniture was still sturdy enough to sit down on. On the wall above the sofa were framed photos of Jesus, Dr. Martin Luther King, Jr. and President John F. Kennedy. She had recently added a formal photo of President Barack Obama to the lineup, as well. On another wall was a collection of family photos, one of which was of me as a toddler.

"Hello," I greeted the elderly woman and the young lady.

"This is Miss Winston and her granddaughter, Lori. They're my neighbors," Grandmother Lorraine announced.

"Nice to meet you," I cordially addressed them while concurrently making eye contact.

"Have a seat right over there and visit with us for a moment." Grandmother Lorraine directed me to an empty seat. I sat down across from Lori and instantly sensed she'd been forced into this awkward visit just as I had been.

"I'm not looking for a girlfriend," I whispered to Lori.

"That's good. Because I'm not looking for a boyfriend," she fired back, releasing a loud sigh and frowning.

"Lori, watch your manners!" Miss Winston seemed appalled by Lori's rudeness. Lori huffed indignantly and seemed to care less about anything her grandmother had to say.

Miss Winston slowly turned her head away from Lori and focused her attention on Grandmother Lorraine. "I don't know what's wrong with these children today, Lorraine. They just don't have any respect whatsoever."

"That's why I'm glad my son and grandson are here with me. The instant my son began having trouble with his ex-wife, I told him to send Wesley to me so I could attend to him while he straightened out his affairs. I would've gotten Wesley in church and would've taught him how to be a good and respectful Christian. If Wesley had come to live with me for a while he would've never gotten into so much trouble." Grandmother Lorraine spoke about me as if I weren't in the room. I gawked at her with a puzzled expression because no one ever mentioned to me that she wanted to take me in. Not that I would've wanted to come, especially since she had such a strict and stern hand.

"Wesley, wipe the ridiculous look off your face. If you open your mouth any wider it's going to fall onto the floor," Grandmother Lorraine admonished. I exhaled loudly out of agitation. "Good, I wanted you to meet Lori. Since the two of you will be going to the same high school, I thought she could help you find your way around." Grandmother Lorraine was suddenly smiling at Lori and me.

"Yes, I think it's an excellent idea if both of you would take some time here today and get acquainted with each other." Both of our grandmothers smiled in our direction as if they had some ulterior motive other than what they were saying. There was a long pause before Grandmother Lorraine suggested to Miss Winston that they grab a cup of coffee in the kitchen. As soon as they exited the room Lori began acting crabby.

"Ooh, that old woman drives me crazy!" Lori grumbled.

"Why? What did she do?" I asked as I curiously studied Lori. She had a cute, oval-shaped face, brown-sugar skin and braided hair. Her thick, black eyebrows gave her a unique and distinguished look, although I could tell it was most certainly time for her to go and get them waxed since there were a lot of fine hairs growing around them. She had a sexy, slender body that teetered on the edge of being too skinny. Her full, succulent lips and small perky breasts added to her attractiveness. Over all she wasn't a bad-looking girl.

"She's being meddlesome and nosy. That old woman keeps trying to control me and everything I do and I'm sick and tired of it!" Lori sprang to her feet and walked over to a window. She pulled back the drapes and glanced outside.

"Listen, Wilson," she said in a frustrated tone.

"Who in the world is Wilson?" I asked.

"That's your name, isn't it?"

"My name isn't Wilson, it's Wesley," I corrected her.

"Whatever." She glanced back out of the window. I'd had just about enough of her and was about to go back downstairs to call Keysha back.

"I'm sorry I got your name wrong. I'm just dealing with a lot of issues right now," she explained in a contrite tone.

"Aren't we all?" I agreed and decided to hold off on leaving her alone since she seemed to have calmed down.

"It's not that hard to figure out how to get around the school. You can read signs posted on a wall, can't you?" Lori asked sarcastically.

"Yes, I can read. I'm not stupid," I shot back at her.

"I never said you were," she quickly answered with a patronizing tone.

"Did I do something wrong? I haven't known you five minutes, but I feel as if we're fighting," I asked, trying to understand why there seemed to be tension between us.

"I don't know, did you do something wrong? I mean, for all I know the FBI could be looking for you at this very moment." Lori opened her purse and removed a stick of chewing gum. She paused then captured my gaze. "Do you want a stick?" she offered.

"No," I answered. "And the FBI doesn't even know my name."

"Well, that's a good thing." She hesitated as she sat back down. "So what classes do you have?"

"Do you really care or are you just asking to make conversation?" I wanted clarification; I was having a difficult time communicating with her.

"If I didn't want to know I wouldn't have asked you." Lori placed the stick of chewing gum in her mouth.

"I don't know what classes I have yet. I have to go up to the school tomorrow and register," I explained as plainly as possible.

"Well, whatever you do, don't let them stick you in any of Mr. Alexander's social studies classes. I had him last semester and he's a real jerk and he loads you up with homework. That guy doesn't have a life. In fact all of the teachers there don't really have a life. It's really tragic when you think about it." Lori reached into her purse once again and removed her cell phone, which was buzzing. I watched her press several buttons and read the text message she'd just received.

"I swear this boy is driving me up a wall." She stuffed her phone back into her purse.

"Got troubles with your man?" I asked mockingly.

"Nothing I can't handle. He's just a little possessive— likes to know my every move, which at first I thought was kind of cute, but now it's just annoying as hell. He follows me around like some crazed stalker on Twitter trying to hook up with a celebrity."

"Sounds like your boyfriend is a real control freak," I affirmed, wanting to pry into her romantic life just out of curiosity. "What else has he done?"

"So who are you? A graduate of the Dr. Phil University of getting into other people's business?" Lori turned snippy in the blink of an eye. I could tell she was the type of person who blurted whatever was on her mind before she placed any thought into how she'd be perceived.

"I don't even watch Dr. Phil, but if dude doesn't like to give you space to breathe, that could spell trouble for your relationship," I answered, genuinely trying to help her. Lori didn't confirm or deny my doubts about the stability of her romantic life. Instead she twisted the conversation around and began asking me questions.

"So what's your story? Where are you from?" she asked.

"Illinois. I live in a suburb called South Holland," I answered.

"Really?" Her mood seemed to change instantaneously.

"Yes, really." I wondered why her attitude had once again done a one-hundred-eighty-degree turn.

"My dad lives there. I spend the summer months in South Holland," she said, using a friendlier tone. "You ever hang out at River Oaks Mall or go to the Tricked Out nightclub?" Lori asked as she draped one leg over the other.

"Yeah, I've hung out at both of those places. I used to live at the night club," I admitted.

"You know, now that I'm looking at you, your face seems familiar." Lori's unyielding stare made me feel awkward.

"You've probably seen me around the neighborhood or just hanging out at Mr. Submarine or something. So will you be going to see your dad this summer?" I asked.

"Yes, I will. Then I'll have to deal with all of his rules. God, I hate rules. There should be a new law banning them," Lori whined as she once again opened her purse, removed a compact mirror and began fussing with her hair.

"Well, if that happened our society would become very chaotic," I pointed out.

"So what are you? The social conscience of America now?"

"Boy, you're really a feisty one, aren't you?" I asked, releasing a phony laugh.

"I'm bossy, feisty, spunky and sometimes quarrelsome. It takes a certain kind of man to handle me."

"Oh, yeah, and what type of man would that be?" I asked, folding my arms across my chest and shifting my weight to sit more comfortably. I wanted to know what type of dude could subdue a nutcase like her.

"A thug. A man who takes charge and is in command. A man who isn't afraid of anything or anyone. Someone completely different from you, obviously." Lori pulled out her cat claws with her last comment.

"Oh, no, you didn't just call me a punk." I chuckled. "You clearly don't know much about me at all."

"Please! You look like you still need to sleep in your bedroom with your night-light on." She smirked with un-wavering conviction.

"Huh. That's a laugh. You shouldn't judge a book by its cover," I said, defending myself.

"I can't help it. That's just the way I am. I can take one look at a person and immediately know if I'm going to be able to get along with them."

"Well, it sounds as if you need to work on yourself some more."

"Tell me something that I don't know. I've already come to the realization that I'm a masterpiece that's still being painted. Only those with a keen eye can really appreciate my beauty."

"I hope heaven broke the mold when they made you," I said, getting ready to leave. I couldn't deal with her conceited arrogance.

"Heaven probably did," she answered vainly, completely ignoring my insult.

"Has anyone ever told you that you're crazy?" I asked.

"I hear it all the time, honey." She tucked the mirror back in her pocketbook, then retrieved a fingernail file. "You know I don't want to be here, right?" Lori admitted as she buffed her nails.

"Neither do I. So I guess we do have one thing in common," I said as I scratched my head.

Lori reached out and touched my hair. "You should go down to Dino's Barbershop and get a trim before your hair turns into a nappy Afro. I can't stand guys who are in to that retro thing. Leave the big Afros in the seventies, please."

I began laughing out loud because I had noticed some guys were trying to bring that look back.

"There's this boy named Roland Gist at school who always tries to be a trendsetter with his hair. Last week he was wearing an Afro-shag-mullet."

I broke into laughter. "Wow, that's funny."

"Yeah, I've heard crazy stories about Roland... Both of his parents were sent to mental institutions. So in my opinion I don't think the brother is playing with a full deck of cards, if you know what I mean."

"Yeah, as my grandmother would say, I catch your drift," I said. "So what are the rest of the students at the school like?"

"Probably like any other school. You've got your nerds, your thugs, your freaks, the weed smokers, weirdos, popular people, jocks and beautiful people of the world like me." Lori pointed to herself and smiled.

"Okay," I said as I tried to process all of that.

"I'll tell you what. Since I sort of know you from my dad's neighborhood, I'll be nice and show you around. Just don't act like you and I are seeing each other on the sly because I've got a reputation to uphold."

"Trust me, girlfriend. I am just not that into you," I said, setting the record straight.

"Well, not yet anyway. But once you see me in one of my freakum dresses, you'll be drooling over me just like the rest of the boys at school," she stated with confident cockiness. I laughed mockingly at her.

"Oh, my, don't you have an excessively high opinion of yourself? You're a little conceited, don't you think?" I said.

"No, I don't think I'm stuck-up. Why do guys always think a confident woman is a threat? Never mind. I really don't want to hear your answer. Anyway, moving on—I live three doors down in the blue house." Lori reached into her purse, dropped the nail file and removed an ink pen and a small writing pad. "Here is my phone number. Send me a text message once you've registered for all of your classes and we'll go from there."

"Okay," I answered as she ripped a page from the notepad and handed it to me.

I didn't plan on ever talking to Lori again because she was a little too over-the-top for me. Once I'd registered for school the next day I didn't bother sending her a text message because I was able to find my way around the school fairly easily. Although I will admit I did get lost once, but the teacher cut me some slack since I was new.

When the dismissal bell rang, I hustled to my assigned locker to grab my coat and my social studies book. The first class my guidance counselor gave me was social studies with Mr. Alexander. Lori was right. The guy loaded me up with homework on my very first day. I exited the school and located the school bus that would take me back home to my grandmother's house. Although the bus ride was pretty noisy it was uneventful. The bus let me off about a block away from my grandmother's house. As I walked home, I saw Lori getting out of an old, brown Chevy Caprice, shouting obscenities at some guy who was dropping her off. As she walked around the front end of the car, the male driver jumped out and grabbed her. He shoved her against the car and pointed an angry finger in her face.

"I'm Percy goddamn Jones and you're going to give me everything I've got coming to me!" Percy barked at her like a madman. I stopped on the sidewalk and gawked at them.

"You don't own me, fool! You're not my daddy. Now

take your damn hands off of me!" Lori didn't seem intimidated by Percy's harsh words.

"I'm not playing with your bony butt! Don't make me hurt you," Percy warned. I decided it was time to keep on moving. Lori's dispute with her boyfriend was none of my business. As I continued on, I heard the pop of a closed fist hitting flesh. When I turned around I saw Lori's knees buckling beneath her. Percy grabbed her arm and shook her violently as he continued his angry rant.

"You don't play around with me like that! Do you understand what I'm saying?" Percy wasn't letting up.

"Help!" Lori shrieked. "Please somebody, help me!"

"Shut up! Before you make me really hurt you!" Percy slammed her body against the car.

"Wesley! Help me," Lori shouted out to me. I turned back around to keep moving. I did not want to get involved in their squabble.

Percy turned and met my gaze. "Who is that? Is that your other man? Are you creeping around on me? Is that what the damn problem is?" Percy once again slammed Lori's body against the car.

"Wesley, please!" Lori called out once more.

"That weak punk isn't going to help you. He's not man enough to deal with a pimp like me," Percy roared like a lion about to make a kill.

"Wesley, run down the street and get my grandmother. Please," Lori begged as she tried to free herself from his clutches.

"Damn!" I said aloud as I dropped my duffel bag, turned around and made the fateful decision.

"Yo, man. Why don't you just let her go?" I said as I approached them.

"Why don't you mind your own damn business!" Percy glanced over his shoulder at me.

"You know it's not right to hit on girls, man. Just let her go," I said, hoping I'd talk some sense into him.

"I'm telling you right now, dog. If you don't back the hell up and get out of my business, I'm going to—"

"Never mind, man. I'll just call the police." I pulled my cell phone out of my back pocket. No sooner had I put it up to my ear than Percy rushed over to me and slapped it out of my hand. He stood menacingly in front of me. Percy was mean and ugly with yellow teeth and bad breath. There was a scar below his left eye and a tattoo on his neck. He was bigger than me, taller than me and as aggressive as a wild pack of hyenas fighting over a fresh kill.

"I told you to move the hell on!" Percy shoved me so hard I almost fell.

"Don't push on me!" I shouted and shoved him back.

"Percy, stop it!" Lori tried to step in. "He doesn't know you. He's new around here. Just let it go!" Lori pleaded.

Percy swung at me, but I saw it coming and moved out of the way of his vicious swing. I immediately coiled my fingers into a tight fist and prepared to throw down.

"You don't want to fight me," I said as I stood my ground, ready to defend myself.

"Too late now," Percy said and unexpectedly rushed toward me, trying to knock me off balance and pin me down on my back. I countered his move by pushing down forcefully on the back of his head while simultaneously raising my knee to meet his face. The impact made a loud thudding sound and stopped Percy cold in his tracks. He collapsed to his knees and covered his face with his hands. Blood began seeping down the back of his hands from his nostrils.

"Stay down, Percy!" I warned him to concede and bring our scuffle to an end.

"Wesley, run! Just run home right now!" Lori hollered.

"You were the one who was begging me for help and now you're telling me to run away?" I was ticked off that I'd even risked getting hurt for her in the first place.

"Wesley, come on! I'm going with you. I'm not defending him," Lori said. Percy removed his hands from his face and looked at the blood on his hands. He then lightly touched his nose, which was swelling rapidly into some deformed shape.

"I think you broke my nose," he said as he continued to gently touch it.

Lori tugged at my arm and pulled me away from Percy, who was just getting to his feet.

"I didn't mean to break your nose. I was just defending myself," I explained. "Let me call for some help so you can get to a hospital," I said, picking up my cell phone.

"I don't need any damn help from you!" Percy said angrily as he staggered over to his car. "This isn't over, boy! This isn't over by a long shot. You'd better pray that the devil gets to you before I do," Percy threatened as I turned my back on him and hurriedly walked away with Lori.

"How are you feeling?" my dad had woken up and was now standing beside my bed.

"Where's Mom?" I asked.

"She's out in the waiting area. Do you want me to get her?"

"No, I don't want to deal with her right now. I don't want to deal with anything."

"Do you remember what happened?" Dad asked.

"No," I answered. "I still don't remember being shot."

five

KEYSHA

It was 7:15 p.m. when I finally finished up my homework. As soon as I was done I did a Google search for hospitals in Indianapolis. Maya held true to her word and looked up a few hospitals for me during her study hall time. I called the places she found during my walk home from school, but none of them had a patient listed under Wesley's name. It was as hard as taking the SAT test when it came to trying to locate Wesley. I continually called his cellular phone, but all I got was his voice mail and I'd left a ton of those. Determined to go see about my man, I feverishly wrote down the names and phone numbers of hospitals on the computer screen, when suddenly I heard a knock on my door. I was concentrating so hard that the noise startled me.

"Jesus, you scared the daylights out of me." I turned and saw Barbara standing at my doorway. I meant to close my door so I wouldn't be disturbed, but in my hastiness to get in the house and get online, I'd forgotten to do that. Barbara wore blue sweatpants with a black top and matching blue-and-black gym shoes. She also had on a pink runners' cap that said Fight Breast Cancer.

"Are you headed out to the workout room above the garage?" I asked, figuring that she'd come to inform me that she'd be stepping out for a while.

"No, I'm actually going to an aerobics class at the community center and I'd like you to join me," she said with a slight smile.

"That's okay, I really don't want to go. I have stuff I need to get done. Go ahead and have a good time." I encouraged her to leave because all I wanted to do was find Wesley.

"Keysha—" Barbara paused "—it's not an option. I want you to change into some workout clothes and come with me." Barbara insisting that I go workout with her was totally lame.

"I had swimming today. I've already had a workout and I don't feel like getting all sweaty and exhausted," I argued.

"It doesn't matter, I still want you to get dressed and come with me."

"Why don't you just take Mike?" I complained, not wanting to be bothered with her at that particular moment.

"Jordan has him cleaning out and reorganizing the garage as part of his punishment. He wanted to punish you as well, but I talked him out of it since we both knew you really had nothing to do with Mike taking Jordan's car." Barbara gave me a sly glance, indicating I owed her a favor. I wanted to scream because she was keeping me from doing what I needed to do.

"Okay." I gave in. "Give me a minute to change my clothes," I said.

"Great! I'll see you downstairs in a few minutes. It will be fun. Besides, you can blow off some steam and get your mind off Wesley," she added.

Get my mind off of him? Honey, I plan on moving heaven and earth to find him and nurse him back to good health, I thought to myself.

Barbara and I went to her step aerobics class, which was filled with middle-aged women trying to recapture their shapely figures that they had allowed to turn into rolls of blubber. The instructor was a woman in her mid-forties who was in phenomenal shape and could easily pass for a woman ten years younger. She gave orders like a drill sergeant and gave a workout that left both Barbara and me barely able to stand.

"Oh, my God!" Barbara said, panting as we exited the aerobics studio and headed back to the locker room. "My legs are hurting so bad right now. I can't believe how out of shape I've gotten."

"Why did you sign up for this class anyway?" I asked as I rubbed my stomach. After we did all of our jumping around, the drill sergeant instructor had everyone get on the floor and work on our abs.

"To get in shape," Barbara answered.

"And?" I pressed the issue because in my mind it had to be more than that. "Is Jordan complaining about your weight or something?"

"No, Jordan isn't complaining about my weight." She

got defensive. "I look very good for my age and damn sexy if I do say so myself," Barbara said with arrogant flair.

"You do look good," I admitted and was about to leave it at that.

"Okay, I'll be honest. My sister is coming to town for a visit in a few weeks and I refuse to allow her to look better than me," Barbara confessed as we both got inside of the car. She fired up the motor and I immediately fiddled with the radio and changed it from Barbara's boring light music station to the top hip-hop station. I stopped when I heard Jennifer Hudson's voice echoing through the speakers.

"Okay, so you're feeling what Jennifer Hudson is saying in this song. You don't feel like being in your sister's spotlight." I chuckled.

"I cannot allow my sister to upstage me. If she thinks for one second that she's—"

"Whoa, time out," I interrupted. "What's the big deal? Why are you competing with your sister like this?"

"Because she doesn't have to work as hard as I do to stay in shape. She's one of those people who can eat anything and not gain a pound. I always want to look younger than her, not older. The last time I saw her she looked fabulous and I looked worn-out. This sibling rivalry between us has been going on for years."

"It seems a little childish at your age, don't you think?" I asked.

"Yes it is, but—" Barbara paused midsentence. I could tell she was really thinking about what I'd just said. "Perhaps you're right, Keysha. Perhaps it's time for us to grow up. Thank you for pointing that out to me." Barbara chuckled.

"Hey, glad I could help," I said.

"I'm a little envious of her, I suppose. After all she's gone through, she's really made a great life for herself." Barbara paused. "Why don't you and I grab a quick bite to eat?" Before I could decline the invitation, Barbara did a quick U-turn and began driving in the opposite direction from home. I wanted to scream, but I held back.

When we finally did get back in the house I ran upstairs to my room and turned the computer back on. As I waited for it to boot up I decided to check in on Mike. I walked down the hall to his room and knocked on the door. When he didn't answer, I took a peep inside. Mike was sprawled on his bed asleep. *Jordan must've worked him like a slave*, I thought to myself as I closed the door.

As I walked back into my room I heard my cellular phone ringing and wondered who was calling me at this late hour. I removed the cell phone from my backpack and saw Maya's name on the display.

"What's going on, Maya?" I asked as I sat at the computer and typed in my password.

"Have you found him yet?" she asked. "I want to know how he's doing if you have."

"No, Maya, I haven't found him yet. I was forced to hang out with my stepmom, but I'm about to get online and continue my search."

"Oh. Well, I won't bother you with my drama then." Maya sounded as if something was really perplexing her. I wanted to say "Cool, I'll talk to you later," but I thought I'd come off as being insensitive.

"What drama?" I asked even though at that point all I really wanted to do was rush her off the phone.

"You have to promise me that you won't tell a soul about this. I'm really trusting you with my secret." Maya was making certain that I understood the magnitude of what she was about to tell me.

"Dang, girl. Is the drama that juicy?" I asked as I stopped what I was doing to give her my complete attention.

"Okay." Maya exhaled and then paused for a long moment. "God, I didn't think talking about this would be so hard, but you're the only person I feel comfortable talking to about it."

"Just say it." I encouraged her to quit stalling.

"I went down to Planned Parenthood today and—"

"Planned Parenthood!" I squawked like a bird fighting over worms after a fresh rain shower.

"Yes and—"

"Maya, hold on a second." I had an incoming phone call and I quickly looked at the caller ID and saw Wesley's name. "Maya, I've got to go. I'll call you back," I said and immediately disconnected her. I didn't even give her a chance to say goodbye. I hung up on her and clicked over to Wesley.

"Wesley, is that you? I've been worried sick about you. And who shot you and why?" I fired off a number of questions. My voice was filled with nervous energy.

"Hello?" an elderly woman spoke.

"Hello? Is this Wesley's grandmother?" I asked, wanting the woman to identify herself.

"Oh, I was just putting Wesley's things away and I

must've pressed the call button by accident. Lord knows I'd never call anyone's house at this late hour."

"It's okay, Miss..." I hoped she'd get the hint to give me her name so I could address her respectfully.

"Who is this?" she asked. *Damn it, old lady! Stick with me here,* I thought.

"My name is Keysha. I'm Wesley's girlfriend. Is he alive? Can you tell me how he's doing?" I asked, pressing her for information.

"Young lady, do you know that it's almost midnight? What are you doing answering the phone at this late hour? You should be in bed or something." I quickly glanced at the clock. It was only 10:45 p.m. *What in the hell is she talking about?*

"It's only ten forty-five. What are you talking about?"

"Oh. You don't live here in Indiana. You're back in Illinois. I forgot we're an hour ahead of you," she explained.

"Okay, time is not what's important right now. I've been up worrying about Wesley and calling around to all of the hospitals in Indianapolis trying to find him," I snapped. She didn't seem to understand the urgency in giving me a medical update on Wesley.

"Oh, Wesley is at the Community Hospital," she answered. "Bless his soul."

"Bless his soul? Oh, my God. Is Wesley dead?" I was fearful of her answer and held my breath while my heart pounded hard against my chest.

"No, he's still living. He's going to be in the hospital a little while longer, but he's going to pull through," she answered.

"Thank God."

"Well, he's not out of the woods just yet. It's going to take him a long time to heal up from that wound."

"What happened? Who shot him and why?" I kept drilling for more information.

"Keysha, that's your name right?" she asked.

"Yes. What's yours? I didn't catch it."

"My name is Ms. Lorraine. Listen, I don't mean to be rude, honey, but I'm very tired. I've been at the hospital all day with him. Just keep Wesley in your prayers for right now."

"Wait. I'm coming to see him. I *have* to see him," I said, desperately wanting to be near him.

"Honey, allow the boy to get well first." I could tell Miss Lorraine didn't want me around, but I didn't care. I was coming to see Wesley no matter what. I was quickly getting the sense that Lorraine was a cranky old woman who didn't particularly care for me, although I didn't know why.

"Did he ask for me?" I wanted to know every detail about Wesley, including the doctor's diagnosis, and when he would be getting out.

"No, but he asked about Lori, though." I heard irritation floating beneath her comment.

"Lori? Who in the hell is Lori?" I swore at her, although I didn't mean to. It was just an immediate reaction to her remark.

"That's his friend. They've gotten really close and he was protecting her when he got shot."

"Wait a minute," I said, trying to process everything I was being told. "Wesley took a bullet for some girl?" I asked just to make sure I'd heard her correctly.

"Listen, precious, I can understand your concern, but I think you need to move on with your life," she said as if my feelings for Wesley could be turned on or off like a light switch.

"Move on?" I blurted out.

"I've been talking to my son about selling his house and moving down here with me, so I can take care of him and Wesley. He's been giving it some serious thought and chances are high they'll remain here with me in Indianapolis."

"I don't believe you. Wesley never said anything about a girl named Lori or staying there and we talked every day. Why are you lying to me? You've never even met me, but I feel as if you hate me. How can you judge me like that?" I asked.

"Keysha, it's been nice talking to you. I'm sorry I called you so late," she answered, totally ignoring my question. "I'll talk to you some other time."

"No, you wait one minute—" I heard a dial tone. "Hello? Are you there?" It only took me a second to realize that I was talking to myself. Miss Lorraine had hung up on me.

"Ooh!" I howled, agitated and flustered. "I'm going to get to the bottom of this mess if it kills me!" I shrieked as I began an inquiry into the cost of a bus ticket to Indianapolis. I discovered that an 8:00 a.m. bus departed from the downtown bus terminal in the morning. The cost of the ticket was ninety-five dollars. I scraped up every penny that I had, but was only able to come up with forty-three dollars. I sat down on the edge of my bed and tried to figure out where I could get the rest of the money without a lot of questions being asked. Then it hit me. "Mike," I said as I popped my fingers and walked down to his room. I opened his door and walked over to his bed. Mike was sleeping flat on his back and snoring loud enough to wake the dead. I forcefully shook his shoulder.

"Mike," I whispered. "Wake up." I shook him harder, but all he did was turn his back to me. "Damn it, Mike! Wake up," I urged, but he did not come to life. I decided to pinch his nostrils shut with my thumb and forefinger. It didn't take him long to wake up gagging for air.

"What's wrong with you, Keysha? What are you trying to do? Kill me?" Mike was pretty peeved that I'd awakened him from his tranquil slumber.

"No, but your breath smells like toxic waste," I said, fanning my hand in front of my nose.

"Go to hell, Keysha." Mike once again turned his back to me. I flipped the switch on a nearby lamp.

"Damn! What do you want?" Mike barked.

"Shh! I need your help with something," I whispered.

"Get with me in the morning. I was having a really good dream and you messed it up. Hopefully I can fall back to sleep and pick up where I left off." Mike pulled his blanket above his head to hide from me.

"Mike, this is life or death. I need your help just like you needed my help to find Jordan's car." I used his guilt trip to get him to listen. Mike huffed as he uncovered his head and sat up in the bed.

"Okay, you win," he said, rubbing his eyes with his fingertips.

"I need some money," I said.

"Money?" Mike asked with a bewildered expression on his face.

"Yes, money. I need to get to Wesley and I don't have enough to cover the bus ticket," I explained as I got up and shut his bedroom door. The last thing I wanted was for Jordan or Barbara to come up the stairs and overhear our conversation.

"Are Mom and Dad okay with you going?" he asked. I answered him with a cynical glare. "Okay. That answers that question. So that means you're going to sneak away to see him."

"Yes," I answered.

"Man, Keysha. I don't know if I want to get involved in this." Mike clearly wasn't getting how urgent this situation was for me.

"Too late. You're already involved. I need two hundred dollars from you," I said.

"Two hundred dollars! Have you lost your mind?" Mike laughed and was about to roll over and go to sleep again.

"Mike, I'm serious. The bus ticket alone is close to one hundred dollars. The other one hundred should cover a cheap motel and cab fare to and from the hospital."

"Keysha, you're not old enough to rent a hotel room," Mike said.

"How do you know?" I asked.

"Trust me on that one. I've tried and as soon as you present an ID that says 'under twenty-one' they're going to tell you that you can't rent a room."

"Fine. Then I'll sleep at the hospital. I'll find a sofa or a chair somewhere and just sleep when I need to."

"Keysha, how are you going to pull this off? You just can't go missing without Barbara or Jordan noticing," Mike said.

"I'll call them when I get there. I'll leave first thing in the morning and call them when they get home from work. They can't stop me from seeing him if I'm already there. I'll deal with the drama and consequences once I see Wesley."

"You know your plan sounds crazy, right?" I could tell Mike was trying to get me to reconsider.

"Yeah, just as crazy as you stealing Jordan's car to go hook up with big-booty Toya," I reminded him.

"Okay, don't remind me. Jordan has been on my back like ink on paper." Mike paused. "If you get caught I'm going to act as if I had no clue about any of this."

"By the time I get caught I'll already be there," I said.

"I just have one question I need answered," Mike said as he scooted over to the other side of the bed. He paused before standing. "What's the big rush to see him? Is he on life support or something?"

"No, but I think he has a new girlfriend he hasn't told me about—and if he does he's going to have hell to pay."

"Keysha, you shouldn't jump to—" Mike stopped talking and then exhaled. "Never mind. I don't have two hundred dollars in cash, but you can take the Visa gift card that I got from Grandmother Katie. It has two hundred fifty dollars on it. I was going to use it to buy video games, but you can have it." Mike went into his closet and rummaged around until he found the card.

"Here you go. Remember, if you get busted I'm not going to go out on a limb for you."

"Don't worry about it. I can handle myself," I reminded him. I gave him a hug for being so generous and then allowed him to get some rest.

I went back into my bedroom and purchased the bus ticket. I printed out my confirmation and then mapped out how I was going to use public transportation to get from my house to the bus terminal downtown. Once I'd figured that out, I packed a small suitcase and left it in a closet near the front door. I planned on getting up extra early to sneak out of the house before anyone woke up. Just so that Barbara and Jordan wouldn't worry, I planned on leaving a note that said I'd left early and I'd call to check in later.

My alarm clock began buzzing early the following morning. I got out of bed as quickly as I could to shut it off. It was five o'clock in the morning and still dark outside. I flirted with the idea of getting back in bed, but I knew that was not an option. As quietly as I could, I maneuvered around the house and got ready. After I grabbed my boarding pass that I'd printed out, I crept downstairs and quietly walked through the house toward the closet where my suitcase was. I set my boarding pass down on a nearby tabletop and wrestled the suitcase out of the closet. Once I had it, I checked my pockets for my door keys and my hip for my cell phone. I opened the door just in time to see the sky open up and unload a heavy downpour of rain. I crept back inside the house and searched the closet until I located an umbrella. As soon as I locked the door behind me, I saw the bus approaching and I made a run for it. I pulled my suitcase along and ran as fast as I could, sloshing through several puddles of water, which immediately soaked through my shoes and wet up my socks. The bus driver saw me running and was kind enough to wait. I was in such a rush to get on the bus that I took a misstep, and hit my head on one of the bus steps.

"Are you okay?" asked the bus driver, who placed the bus in Park and got out of his seat to help me back to my feet.

"I'm okay. I just lost my footing," I said as I got up. That's when I noticed a trail of my clothes on the ground. I quickly checked the suitcase and spotted the broken zipper and cursed. "Could you please hold on for one minute?" I pleaded with the bus driver.

"I'm on a schedule here," the driver complained as I rushed along the curb picking up my wet clothes. I stuffed my belongings back inside the suitcase and then carefully boarded the bus. I paid my fare and found an empty seat. Once I got situated, I exhaled and glanced out of the window as the bus drove past my high school. The bus made several more stops before entering the highway, which would take the morning commuters and myself downtown to the Greyhound bus terminal. The bus hadn't been on the highway a good five minutes before it slowed to a complete stop. I glanced out of the window and noticed traffic on both sides of the highway had come to a stop.

"Damn it, what's the delay?" I uttered under my breath. I looked around at the other commuters, who seemed oblivious to the stalled traffic. Some were reading books, while others were on their cellular phones. I exhaled a frustrated sigh because I didn't want to be late. After sitting still for twenty minutes, the bus driver finally made an announcement.

"Folks, it appears there's a nasty traffic accident ahead of us. It's probably due to the heavy rain. We'll get going again once the state police open the highway back up."

"Agggh!" I growled as I looked at my watch, hoping that we'd get moving soon.

I finally arrived at the bus station at 7:55 a.m. and raced through the bus terminal over to the ticket counter, where I had to stand and wait in a long line to get my boarding pass validated. I finally got to the ticket counter and began searching for my boarding pass. I searched my pockets, but didn't find it. I searched my purse and it wasn't there, either.

"Hang on a minute," I told the ticket agent. "I know I brought it with me." Patting my pockets frantically, I still couldn't locate the ticket. "Damn it!" I exhaled as I stood with my eyes closed.

"Never mind, honey, what's your name? I'll look you up in the system," said the ticket agent. I gave my name and she quickly typed it into the system.

"Oh, dear. You'd better get moving. Your bus will be pulling off any second now." The ticket agent gave me a new boarding pass and pointed in the direction that I needed to go. I scooped up my busted suitcase and made a run for it. My clothes began falling out of the suitcase once again and I tripped over a dangling pants leg and fell. My knees hit the marble floor pretty hard, but I was determined to catch that bus. I hobbled to my feet, gathered my belongings and limped toward my destination. Just as I was about to hand the driver my boarding pass, I heard someone howl out, "Keysha Kendall! Where do you think you're going?" I immediately spun around and saw Jordan rushing toward me with a dissatisfied expression on his face. He'd pulled in his bottom lip and bit down on it and his eyes were fixed on my like a tiger about to deliver a fatal bite.

SIX

WESLEY

I was sitting up in my hospital bed being spoon-fed what had to be the nastiest-tasting soup in the world for breakfast. Grandmother Lorraine was making sure that I ate every drop.

"Come on now, Wesley, stop making this harder than it has to be. How am I supposed to nurse you back to good health if you won't eat?"

"This stuff is horrible," I complained as I slowly swallowed down another spoonful. "What else is there to eat?" I scanned the food tray for something that would perhaps taste better.

"Wesley, you will not eat anything else until you finish this soup!" my grandmother insisted. I smashed the back of my head against my pillow and groaned. Grandmother Lorraine gave me an evil glare, which meant she wasn't playing around with me about eating. I reluctantly gave in to her will and ate the soup.

"Is that stuff any good?" my mother asked as she entered the room with my dad trailing behind her. She was wearing a citrus-yellow dress and red patent-leather high-heeled shoes. Her freshly dyed black hair was pulled back in a tight bun.

"No," I answered immediately.

"I didn't think it was because it doesn't smell good at all."

"At least it smells better than alcohol," Grandmother Lorraine muttered as she moved the bed tray away.

"Whatever!" said my mother as she gave my grandmother a nasty look.

"I'm ready to get out of this place," I whined.

"I know you are." My mother paused. "Wesley, your father and I were talking and I feel that you'd be better off living with me."

"Better off living with you?" Grandmother Lorraine snapped. "I don't think so."

"He's not your son. He's mine," my mother shouted.

"Hey, there is no need to get nasty with each other," my father said, bringing about some order to the tension between them. "Wesley, your mom feels strongly about you going to live with her and I feel that you should stay with me."

"Hold up," I said because I didn't want this conversation to continue. "Mom, I don't want to stay with you. I want to be with Dad."

"But he's not taking good care of you. For God's sake, Wesley, you've been shot," my mother griped.

"And he ended up in jail when he was with you. So

what's your point?" Grandmother Lorraine just couldn't stay out of the argument.

"Dad, seriously, I'd rather stay with you," I stated once again.

"Then that settles it." My father turned to my mother, who wasn't at all happy with my decision.

"He's going to get you killed," my mother said angrily as she turned to leave.

"She didn't mean that, Wesley." Dad tried to clean up her comment.

"Yes, she did," I said without empathy. I'd turned off my feelings for my mother a long time ago and I certainly wasn't about to turn them back on now. There was a knock at the door and I turned my head and saw two uniformed police officers enter.

"Hello, everyone, I hope you remember us. I'm Officer Davis and this is my partner, Officer Miles." Both men approached my bedside.

"How are you feeling, partner?" Officer Davis asked. My pulse inexplicably quickened. The monitor tracking my heart rate began to beep.

"Relax, Wesley. We're only here to ask you some questions about the shooting," Officer Davis explained, but I still didn't feel at ease.

"Can't you do this some other time?" Grandmother Lorraine asked.

"No, ma'am. We really need to talk to him," Officer Davis stated adamantly. "We have a pretty heavy caseload and we have to turn in a report on this case."

"Wesley—" Officer Davis pulled out an ink pen and

notepad "—in your own words, tell me what happened."
I was silent for a brief period as I tried to reconstruct everything that had taken place.

"I don't know," I said as I turned my head and glanced out of the window. "I got shot."

"We know that much," said Officer Davis. "What we need to know is who shot you and why?"

"I don't want to say," I answered.

"Wesley, tell the man who shot you." Dad took my hand into his own. "It's okay."

"I don't want to be a snitch," I explained.

"Are you involved in a gang?" asked Officer Davis.

"No, my son isn't involved with gangs," my dad spoke up for me.

"Sir, I need to hear it from Wesley," Officer Davis said firmly. "Wesley, are you involved with any gang?" he asked once again.

"It all depends on what you consider to be involved," I answered.

"Wesley! I know you haven't run off and joined a gang since you've been here!" Dad shouted at me.

"Sir, please, allow him speak," Officer Davis insisted.

"No, Dad, I haven't done anything like that," I answered.

"Are you sure?" Officer Davis pressed the issue.

"I'm positive," I answered, then closed my eyes tightly as images of the incident began to flash in my mind.

"Have you had any altercations with gang members?" asked Officer Davis.

"I've gotten into a few fights," I answered, feeling as if I was under an enormous amount of pressure.

"Okay. Can you give some details?"

"About which fight? I've had a few of them."

"Why don't you start from the beginning, so I have the full picture?" He stood poised and ready to take down notes.

"You'd better pull up a chair," I suggested. Officer Davis and Officer Miles did just that. My dad leaned against the wall and Grandmother Lorraine sat down on the empty patient bed. I took a few deep breaths.

"I didn't want to get involved with Lori and her boyfriend," I said.

"So are you involved in some type of romantic love triangle?" asked Officer Davis.

"I don't know. At least I don't think I am. I mean, Lori and I have sort of a love-hate relationship. She's a bossy girl, but once you get around her defenses, she's really nice," I explained.

"So, the shooting is over a girl named Lori?" Officer Davis wanted to be sure he was getting all of the facts correct.

"Yeah, man, it's all over a girl." I paused and then explained how I'd come to Lori's rescue one afternoon when her boyfriend was beating her up.

"So after the fight, what happened next? Did her boyfriend try to get even with you?" Officer Davis began scribbling on his notepad.

"After the fight I walked Lori to her front gate. Percy had hit her so hard that her right eye had begun to swell shut. I wanted to call the paramedics, but she insisted she was fine and didn't need any help. She pleaded with me to keep my mouth shut about the entire incident. I thought it was kind of strange, but I let it go because I just didn't feel it was any of my business and I didn't want to get involved any more than I already had. Lori went inside and I came home and chilled out. I have to admit that I was nervous about retaliation, but when I didn't see Percy for an entire week I took it as a sign that he wasn't coming after me. Then two weeks later, I ran in to Percy and his crew on the school bus. I don't even know why he was on my school bus. He just showed up. I didn't want any trouble with them, so I avoided him and his crew and sat down in my usual seat." My mind wandered back to the images of that day.

"You're sitting in my seat!" Percy had come up to me, clearly wanting to throw down.

"I don't see your name written on this seat," I said, unafraid, as I glanced up at his broken nose.

"Who you rollin' with?" he asked, but I didn't respond. "I knew you were with somebody that day when I first ran in to you at the grocery store. Do you remember what I told you? I said if I found out you were in any other gang I was going to put you six feet under."

"I told you then and I'm telling you now—I represent God."

"Church boys don't know how to break a man's nose, only gangbangers do. You know this is ass-whipping day, don't you?" he said through clenched teeth.

The next thing I knew, it quickly turned into a brawl and I was defending myself against Percy and two of his friends. When all was said and done I had a cut over my left eye and a split lip. During the scuffle I ended up issuing a black eye and knocking out Percy's incisor tooth. Since Percy and his boys started the fight, they got suspended.

My dad was now standing with his hands on his hips. His brow was wrinkled and his mouth was set in a grim line. "Wesley, you told me that you got hit with a ball during gym class. You said that's how you got the cut over your eye and the split lip." My dad was clearly upset about the lie I'd told.

"I didn't want you to worry about me. You had enough to deal with. I didn't want to dump something like this on you," I explained.

"Wesley, you should've come to me. We could've notified the school about it." My dad continued to fuss at me.

"I'm sorry, okay?" I stopped talking because my throat was dry. "Can I have some water please?" Grandmother Lorraine quickly got up and filled up a white foam cup with water and handed it to me. I lifted my head off the pillow and took a few gulps before relaxing once again.

"Go on. What happened next?" Officer Davis asked.

"Nothing happened after that. Percy and his goons were suspended. I didn't see them anymore and that was perfectly fine with me."

"What about the girl? When did you see her again?"

"She'd heard about the fight so she dropped by to see how I was doing. I wasn't really hurt, but she felt guilty about asking for my help and everything that happened afterward. She said she wanted to thank me for helping her get away from Percy. I told her it was no big deal and she didn't have to repay me, but she insisted. She wanted to take me out for pizza. I was in an awkward position.

I really wanted to say no, but the pleading look in her eyes made me say yes."

"So you went on a date with her?"

"I really wouldn't call it a date. We just went to a nearby pizza parlor. We actually had a pretty decent time. I learned a lot about her. I learned who she truly was and all the difficult times she was going through."

"Stuff like what?" Officer Davis asked, digging for more information.

"Family drama. She told me her grandmother had been physically abused by her grandfather for years. Miss Winston never left her husband. She stayed in the marriage and dealt with the punishment. Lori's mother grew up watching all of the abuse and felt that a man didn't truly love a woman unless he beat on her. Lori's father never raised a hand to her or her mother, which her mom took as a sign that there was no love in their marriage. Her mom ended up having an affair with a physically abusive man. Eventually her mother's lover confronted Lori's dad and things got messy. After a nasty divorce, Lori and her mother moved in with her grandmother, Miss Winston."

"So Lori and Miss Winston think it's okay for a man to beat up on them?" Grandmother Lorraine muttered. She was without a doubt awestruck by the discovery of this news.

"Grandma, I told Lori she didn't have to follow in her mother's or grandmother's footsteps. I told her it wasn't cool to stay with a dude who beats up on women. Lori then said that ever since she was a little girl, whenever a little boy hit her, her mom told her it was okay because that's the way little boys show their affection."

"Well, I'll be damned," my father uttered as if that was the oddest thing he'd ever heard.

"So you got to know Lori over a few slices of pizza. What happened after that?" Officer Miles had asked a question for the first time. I took a deep breath and continued.

"Well, while Lori and I were eating pizza, talking and laughing, Percy and his crew walked in. When he saw us he walked over to our table. Percy had nothing but hate in his heart for me and accused me of screwing around with her behind his back. I told him it wasn't like that, but Lori set Percy off by suggesting that she and I were hooked up."

"Why would she say such a thing?" my dad asked.

"I don't know. I think she just wanted to get even with him." I shrugged. "Percy then lifted his shirt and exposed the handle of a gun." I paused and buried my face in my hands. I was having a horrible flashback.

"Wesley, are you okay?" Dad asked.

"I hate him!" I said angrily. "I can't believe this happened to me."

"Wesley, I can appreciate how difficult it is to talk about this. But I really need you to finish telling me what happened."

"I'm not sure what happened. I keep getting flashes of images from the shooting," I explained.

"Here, drink some more water. Take a few deep breaths and try to relax." Officer Davis grabbed the water pitcher and refilled my cup. The cold water helped to calm my nerves, and a few minutes passed before I began talking again.

"Percy said that he was going to shoot both of us. I tried to reason with him, but it was no use. Percy cocked the hammer back and I saw the belly of the gun rotate but just then a police officer walked in. Percy backed off and left."

"Why didn't you or Lori report him to the officer who'd walked in?" asked Officer Miles.

"I don't know. Neither one of us were thinking about reporting anything. I just wanted to go home and so did she. Once we were certain Percy and his goons were gone, we left. During the walk home, Lori once again apologized for getting me involved in such a mess. She also explained that Percy was not only crazy, but he was also a well-known gang member. If Percy says he's going to shoot you, he means it. Lori made that very clear. I tried not to be afraid of him, but deep down inside I knew we would meet again, and it wasn't going to end peacefully. During our walk back home, Lori looped her arm through my own and held on to me. She admitted how frightened she had become of Percy. She said that he'd hit her before, but he always made her feel as if she had it coming because of her bossy ways. I just listened as she talked. When she didn't feel like sharing any more details she rested her head against my shoulder. Once we arrived at her gate, she kissed me. That was the last thing I'd expected from Lori. I embraced her and tried to reassure her everything was going to work out. Then, I heard the sound of a car door slam. I turned around and saw Percy walking toward us wearing a black bandanna that covered his nose and face. I shielded Lori with my body just before Percy pulled out his gun and fired multiple rounds. I don't remember what happened after that."

"Was there anyone else with Percy?" Officer Davis asked as he continued to take notes.

"I don't know," I answered.

"Will you testify in court?" He put away his pen and pad.

"Of course he will. I'm sure Lori's family will testify as well," Dad said.

"I wouldn't count on that. Ms. Lori Brown and her mother are fearful of retaliation and have refused to help us in our investigation," Officer Davis explained.

"You're kidding, right?" I asked.

"I wish I was…. The state prosecutor will look at our report and determine whether or not to press charges. In the meantime, I'll go back to the station and have a warrant issued for the arrest of Percy Jones. We'll bring him in for questioning and go from there. If you can convince Ms. Brown to testify, it would help a great deal. Get well soon." Officer Davis rose to his feet and exited the room with Officer Miles trailing behind him.

seven

KEYSHA

when Jordan found me at the bus station, I impulsively ran away from him. I plowed through the crowded terminal, determined to escape the punishment that awaited me. Needless to say I couldn't run very fast or get very far with a busted suitcase. When he caught me, I wasn't in my right mind and fought him off by swinging my fists and punching him several times in the chest.

"Let me go!" I shrieked as I continually assaulted him with a barrage of jabs. When I realized my strikes were ineffective, I slapped Jordan and tried to shred his face apart with my fingernails. I was determined to be by Wesley's side one way or another. I fought Jordan so vigorously that other passengers in the terminal thought he was attacking me.

"Keysha, if you hit me again you will cause me to commit child abuse and you'll never see Wesley again!" Jordan barked. By the tone of his voice I knew he meant business. Before I realized it, a security guard had rushed over to see what my hysterics were all about.

"She's my daughter and she's trying to run away," Jordan quickly explained as he held on to my wrists to keep me from swinging at him anymore.

"Ma'am, is this true?" asked the security guard, who'd removed a can of pepper spray, aimed it at Jordan's face and placed his thumb on the trigger. I glared at the guard for a hot minute with tears in my eyes. Then without any further explanation, I gave up.

"Let me go, please," I mumbled, surrendering completely to my father. Jordan released me and I sat down on a nearby bench. Feeling overwhelmed, embarrassed and disgraced, I vainly willed myself not to cry.

"Ma'am, is this man your father?"

"Yes, he's my dad and he's not hurting me," I answered.

"I need to handle this. Can you give us some privacy?" Jordan spoke directly to the guard, who was hesitant about stepping away. "Seriously, give us some privacy," Jordan said once again, as politely as he could under the circumstances.

"Are you sure you're okay, miss?" the guard asked once again just to be absolutely certain.

"Yes, I'm fine," I answered as I waved him away. A massive headache had developed near the back of my head. Jordan stooped down and picked up my clothes, which had spilled out of the suitcase once again during my feeble attempt to flee from him. Once he'd collected everything he said, "You inadvertently left your boarding pass at the house." I knew Jordan wasn't happy about the decision I'd made, but it was my choice, not his.

"I forgot it when I rushed out of the house this morning," I admitted as I buried my face in my hands.

"Come on. It's time to go someplace where we can talk about this." In spite of everything I'd just done, Jordan didn't raise his voice or chew me out. He was calm, cool and collected.

"Are you hungry?" he asked.

"No!" I answered defiantly. I knew it was wrong to have an attitude with him, but I couldn't help it. I wasn't able to do what I wanted to do and that true fact annoyed me.

"Do you want me to get ugly with you, because I certainly can?" My smart-aleck remark had ruffled Jordan's feathers.

"No," I muttered.

"What? I can't hear you?" Jordan pressed the issue.

"No," I answered loud enough for him to hear.

"That's what I thought you said. We're going to stop and have breakfast." He extended his hand and helped me to my feet. I followed him to the car, wondering how I was going to get to Wesley.

Jordan headed west toward a location known as Greek Town. Neither one of us said anything during the short drive. The silence inside the car was louder than any heated argument I'd ever heard. The hushed tension between us moved like a slow-burning wick of an explosive device, just waiting to reach the gunpowder and blast.

Jordan pulled into the parking lot of a small breakfast place I'd never been to. There were several blue-and-white police squad cars in the parking lot and I intuitively knew it was a popular spot with cops. Not wanting to look at Jordan, I focused on a homeless woman approaching us, pushing a shopping cart filled with all of her belongings. There was nothing interesting about her, so I turned my head slightly and focused on a cluster of pigeons squabbling over scraps of food on the ground near a Dumpster. At that moment I wished I were a pigeon with no worries and nothing better to do other than eat crumbs.

"Let's go sit inside and talk." Jordan opened the door and stepped his foot onto the concrete.

"I don't want to!" I snapped at him. I wasn't hungry nor was I in the mood for one of Jordan's self-righteous lectures. I just wanted to go back to the bus terminal, get on the bus and go see Wesley. Why Jordan didn't understand the urgency of the hour was beyond my understanding.

"Okay. Then we'll sit here and talk." Jordan locked the car door and positioned himself so that he was looking directly at me. "I want you to hear me crystal clear, Keysha. I am not going to allow you or Mike to give me a coronary, so I'm going to give it to you straight and raw just like I've been giving it to Mike. All of your sneaking around is unacceptable. If you want the privileges of an adult then it's time for you to leave my house and head out into the world on your own. If that's what you want then let me know so I can pack up the rest of your belongings." Jordan was trying to play hardball and scare me, but I didn't believe a single word coming out of his mouth. After all that he'd gone through to make sure I stayed in the house with him, I felt pretty confident that he wasn't going to suddenly change course and turn his back on me.

He tried to entice me once again with the offer of total freedom. "Just give me the word, Keysha, and you can go." I looked directly in his eyes, searching to see if he truly meant what he was saying. After a long minute of silence, I sensed that he was just bluffing.

"Are you saying that you don't want me anymore?" I called his bluff.

"You have to live by my rules, Keysha. I've been giving you the benefit of the doubt and cutting you a lot of slack because I didn't raise you. But right here and right now, I'm drawing the line and giving you an option. You're welcome to stay, but my rules must be followed. No more sneaking around, no more dishonesty and no more running away. You are to go to school, get good grades, do your chores, be respectful and most important of all, stop getting into trouble. If you can't abide by those simple rules, then the door is wide open and you can walk out." Jordan leaned over and opened up the car door on my side to prove his point. "You can walk back to the bus station and go to Wesley, but if you do, that really says to me that you no longer want my help and you don't want to be with the family any longer."

I thought about my next move and concluded that Wesley needed me and nothing was going to stop me from getting to him. I knew Jordan would never understand, so I didn't bother trying to explain it to him.

"Whatever! You don't own me! You can't tell me what to do! I've been taking care of myself ever since I was a little girl. I didn't need you then and I don't need you now! I can make it on my own. No, Wesley and I can make it on our own. We love each other and nothing on this earth can ever break my love for him. Not you, not Justine or anyone else for that matter!" I snarled with defiant igno-rance. I felt as if I'd put him in his place by telling him exactly what I thought. Then I pulled out my suitcase from the backseat, got out of the car and began walking back toward the bus terminal. As I walked away, I noticed the homeless woman stop at the Dumpster and shoo all of the pigeons away. They flew above my head and I ducked because I didn't want to get hit with pigeon droppings. Once the birds were gone, I focused on the homeless woman once again. She opened up the Dumpster lid and began searching for food. I watched as she removed a white foam container and ate a crust of bread that some-one had taken several bites out of. I then looked back at Jordan, who'd gotten out of the car.

"Keysha!" he called to me, but I quickened my pace because I didn't want to hear a word that he had to say. "Keysha!" he called out once again. By that time, I'd flagged down a cab. As soon as I got situated I told the driver where to go. "Pull off, please," I urged. The driver immediately made a U-turn and sped off in the direction of the bus terminal.

eight

WESLEY

The following morning I was wheeled out of my room so a series of X-rays could be taken. Once completed, I was transported back to my quarters, where my breakfast was waiting on me. I scooted back into bed, got comfortable and began eating. Being restricted to a hospital was a drag. I was ready to go home. But more importantly, I was eager to find Lori to talk some sense into her. I had a difficult time comprehending why she refused to cooperate with police, especially after all of the mayhem Percy caused. I understood her being afraid, but this wasn't the time to turn into a yellow chicken. At least it wasn't from my perspective. I could hardly wait to go to court and put Percy behind bars for what he'd done to me.

"Ahhh," I groaned as my right arm began twitching violently. It ached so badly I moaned again. I tried to cope by breathing hard and grinding down on my teeth. It was difficult to manage the pain, but I was determined to bear it while waiting for the excruciating episode to pass. Dr. Foxx explained earlier that sudden sensations of discomfort were a part of the healing process. My distress was so horrific it caused me to have a flashback. I immediately remembered the scent of my burning skin when the red-hot bullet bored through me. I recalled trying to brace myself before I hit the ground and even recollected the haunting sound of my skull slamming against the concrete. I slapped myself on the head a few times with my left hand as if hitting myself would rid my mind of the recurring memory. I willed myself to focus on something else, but it was difficult. Then, I had a revelation and reached for the television remote. I turned on the television just in time to catch an episode of *Family Guy*. I watched the program and laughed loudly at the antics of baby Stewie. Just as the program ended, there was a knock at my door. When I looked up I was surprised to see Lori. I smiled as I turned off the television.

"Hey," she greeted me as she approached my bed.

"Where have you been?" I asked.

"Around," she answered as she removed her jacket and placed it on a nearby coat hook. "How are you feeling?"

"My pain comes and goes, but overall I'm doing well considering how everything went down." I repositioned my bed by adjusting the height knob, so I could see her better. She looked great. Nice jeans, formfitting top and hair styled nicely. I noticed her succulent lips and the pretty red lipstick she'd applied.

"I know. That was crazy, wasn't it?" she asked, agreeing with me.

"Crazy is an understatement." I laughed a little. "So what's up with you not wanting to help the police convict Percy?" I asked flat out.

"It's complicated, Wesley." She paused. "Let's not talk about it right now, okay? I had to jump through a lot of hoops to get here to see you. I had to lie, steal money from beneath my grandmother's mattress and sneak out of the house. I'm so glad you're going to be okay. I truly am." Lori leaned forward and hugged me. I embraced her with my left arm while she simultaneously kissed my forehead.

"You've got to testify, Lori," I tried to persuade her because it was important to me.

"Shhh, baby." Lori placed her index finger up to my lips. "Can I say thank you first? What you did was so brave and heroic. You literally took a bullet for me and saved my life. Wesley, I'll always be grateful to you for doing that. If you had not pushed me out of the way and stepped in front of me, I would probably be dead right now. No one has ever protected me the way you have. I feel so safe when I'm near you."

"I can see why. Especially if I'm the one absorbing all of the bullets that are meant for you," I said.

"I know, sweetie, and I promise you I'll make it up to you. Whatever it takes I'll be there for you. I'll help you with your work at school. I'll help you get well…I'll be at your service, Wesley." Lori tenderly caressed the side of my face. I held her gaze for a moment and could see that she was thinking about something really hard.

"You're my Superman," she whispered and then leaned in to kiss my lips. When our lips met, I tried not to enjoy it. I wanted to resist, but the tasty sweetness of her soft lips caused my body to betray me. I surrendered to her. Lori then placed her sweet kisses on my cheeks and neck.

"Doesn't that feel better?" Lori spoke deliberately in my ear like Aphrodite, the goddess of love tempting a new boyfriend. I was somewhere between confused and horny and would agree with anything she said.

"Yeah. That was nice," I admitted as I tried to understand why and how we were heading down the road of intimacy. Common sense told me to beware of Lori, however my hormones were unmistakably energized about the possibility of more kisses.

"Let me help you eat your food." Lori picked up the knife and fork on the tray and began to cut up my food into smaller portions.

"My mother is acting crazy," Lori confessed. "When the police came to talk to me, my mother freaked completely out, especially when the police told her Percy was a gangbanger. She thinks you're one, as well."

"Why does she think I'm a gangbanger? I'm the furthest thing from that. I don't wear sagging pants or have tattoos. I don't walk around with a gun in my pocket or have a criminal record." I got upset because of how I was being perceived.

"It's complex, Wesley." Lori lifted some food up to my mouth and began to feed me.

Once I chewed my food I said, "It's not difficult at all. Percy shot at us because he thought we were dating. It's a clear-cut case of jealousy."

"That part is." Lori smiled slyly.

"What do you mean by that?" I asked, eyeing her suspiciously and suspecting she was eluding some bigger secret that I knew nothing about.

Lori exhaled and remained silent. "Promise you won't get mad at me?" Lori asked.

"Get mad at you for what?" I was confused, but wanted to know where she was going with the conversation.

"Wesley, first off, I'm not even supposed to be dating. I'm not allowed to have a boyfriend. I was sneaking around with Percy behind my mother's back. I think my grandmother knew, but I can't be certain."

"What does that have to do with you testifying?" I asked.

"Wesley." Lori paused again. "I provoked Percy."

I sat up as tall as I could. "What did you just say to me?" I asked, not sure if I wanted her to repeat what she'd just said.

"When I asked you to go out with me for pizza I knew Percy was going to show up. I told him that you and I would be there." Lori lowered her eyes in shame.

"Why in the hell did you do that?" I shouted, feeling my aggravation mounting.

"Revenge, Wesley. I wanted to get payback. I wanted to crush his ego and teach him a lesson. I told him stuff— told him I'd given it up to you…even told him that I let you put it in without a condom. He'd been trying to get me to get down with him for the longest, but I wouldn't and that frustrated him. That's why we were fighting in the car that day. He was forcing himself on me. He kept trying to get between my legs. He wanted to do me right there in his car in broad daylight. He was rough and aggressive and wouldn't take no for an answer. I told him I wasn't ready and he should respect me, but Percy didn't want to hear it. All he wanted was some sex. He tried to force my head down between his thighs, so that I'd give him oral sex, but the very thought of it made my stomach turn. I fought him off and jumped out of the car. That's when he lost it and decided to beat me down. Anyway, after you helped me, he kept calling me. I wanted the phone calls to end, so I figured if I told him you belonged to another gang back in Chicago and that you were going to kick his ass again, he'd leave me alone. I made stuff up just to get my vengeance. I had no idea Percy would bring a gun with him to the pizza parlor. I had no idea that he'd even do something as crazy as try to murder us. I never intended for any of this to happen."

"This entire situation is—"

"Wesley, I know I've messed up," Lori interrupted. "Please don't yell at me because I can't take being shouted at right now. Yelling at me would just crush me right now. I just want to make things right between us. I want you to know that I'm sorry and that I'm forever indebted to you."

"You need to work with the police and testify, Lori," I said, wanting to win my argument of helping the police bring Percy to justice.

"Wesley, you're not understanding. My mother won't let me testify because she's afraid of retaliation. She doesn't want me to have anything to do with this. She's too afraid. She didn't even want me to come here to see you because she fears that Percy and his goons will come in here and just start shooting up the place."

"Lori, if you don't stand up now and this guy gets off, he'll continue to harass you."

"I know." Lori paused in thought. "I'll do it, Wesley. I'll have to find some way to keep this from my mother, but I'll do it."

"Good, because it's the right thing to do," I said, feeling more at ease now that I'd talked some sense into her.

"So we'll go through this together, right?" Lori asked.

"Of course," I answered. "Come here," I said, reaching up to embrace her. Lori allowed me to hug her and I whispered, "It's going to be okay. Sometimes doing the right thing is hard to do." We held on to each other for some time before I let her go.

"You know, I was thinking." Lori fed me more of my food. "You're a really good kisser and you're not a bad-looking guy. You're nicer than most guys and I'm glad that you haven't tossed me out of the room for what I've done."

"I don't want to talk about it anymore," I said.

"Okay, but I just wanted to let you know that your kisses are so sweet and I would love to be your girlfriend."

"Lori—"

"Don't say anything. Just think about that and let me take care of you," she said as she placed more food in my mouth. We looked at each other for a while, then I smiled at her warmly.

"Wesley, is that you?" the sound of Keysha's voice startled me. I looked past Lori and was super shocked to see Keysha standing in the doorway. I quickly swallowed my food.

"What are you doing here?" I asked.

"Oh, my God, it is you!" Keysha positioned her suitcase

against the wall and rushed over to my bed. "I'm so happy that I've finally found you." Keysha seemed overjoyed but I could tell right away that something was slightly off.

"Are you hurting? Is there anything I can do for you?" Keysha asked a number of questions. She appeared to be overly eager to help me in any way she could.

"He's okay. I'm taking good care of him," Lori spoke up as she gave Keysha a judgmental glare.

"Who are you?" Keysha asked defensively.

"I'm––"

"Keysha, how did you get here?" I cut Lori off before she could answer.

"It's a long story, Wesley, and I don't want to talk about it right now. All I know is I wasn't about to allow you to sit in this hospital all alone. I knew you'd want me to come. I knew that you'd want me to be here with you. I could feel it in my heart," Keysha said as she rubbed my leg and then my bare feet. "I couldn't sleep at night knowing that you'd been hurt."

"How did you even find out?" I asked, still dumbfounded as to how she'd gotten here.

"Your grandmother told me," she said.

"And once your parents found out, they drove all the way here so that you could see me?" I asked, figuring I'd pieced together the scenario that got her here.

"Not exactly," Keysha answered as she continued to rub my feet.

"What do you mean, 'not exactly'?"

"Yes. What do you mean?" Lori asked as she moved my food tray out of the way.

"Are you his nurse or something?" Keysha asked Lori, looking her up and down.

"No, I'm not," Lori answered.

"Then can you, like, excuse yourself or something while I talk to my man?" Keysha rolled her eyes and became deliberately snotty with Lori.

"Oh, hell no! Hold up, chick! You don't come up in here telling me what to do," Lori snapped.

"Wesley, who is she?" Keysha asked, her voice rising. I looked into Keysha's eyes and could see that she was in a very feisty, "take no prisoners" kind of mood.

"Keysha, this is Lori. She's a friend," I answered truthfully.

"So you're the whore." Keysha gave Lori a nasty glare as she folded her arms across her chest.

"Slut, you don't even know me!" Lori barked back, matching Keysha's fire with her own.

"I know enough about you to know that I don't like you." Keysha didn't hold back for one instant.

"Hold on, you two. Stop it before things get out of hand." I tried to cool the tension between them. It was clear, at least from what I was witnessing, that Keysha and Lori were heading down the slippery slope of a girl brawl.

Lori postured defiantly, raised her right arm high above her head and pointed two fingers and her thumb at Keysha as if she were shooting a gun. "How are you just going to come up in here and start calling people out of their name?" Lori ignored what I'd just said about calming down and was sharpening her claws for a catfight.

"Wesley's grandmother told me all about you." Keysha sized Lori up once again and then cautiously turned back to look at me. "What I want to know, Wesley, is why is she even here and how did you get shot over her?" Keysha rudely pointed her index finger close to Lori's face.

"You'd better get your damn fingers out of my face before I chop them the hell off!" Lori threatened.

"Oh, I can't believe this is happening," I said, not wanting to deal with this type of drama.

"Well, Wesley? Is it her or is it me that you're in love with?" Keysha asked flat out as she lowered her hand and glanced sideways at Lori.

"Keysha, you're overreacting," I said, trying to calm her down. I tried to move but I felt a sharp pain and opted to stay put.

"Hmph! Obviously he isn't in love with you the way you think he is. He hasn't smiled once since you've walked in the door," Lori pointed out.

"I don't think anyone was talking to you, tramp!" Keysha snapped.

"Hey! That's enough!" I yelled at them both. "Keysha, where are you staying?" I asked.

"She needs to leave the room. I'm not saying anything until this heifer gets out," Keysha growled. I'd never seen this side of her. She was acting like a person who was unstable.

"I'm not going anywhere," Lori said.

"Would you two please cut it out? You guys don't even know each other and you're squabbling like cats and dogs." I once again pleaded with them to be civil toward each other.

"She started it," Lori said.

"And I'll damn sure be the one to finish it," Keysha

taunted Lori. She certainly wasn't behaving like the Keysha I knew—the one who needed to be rescued.

"Keysha, what's going on? You don't seem like yourself." I didn't want to seem like I was interrogating her, but I couldn't help it.

"Do you have any idea of what I did to get here? I risked everything to be here at your side. I'd hoped you'd be here resting comfortably while waiting for me to arrive. I pictured you telling me how much you loved me and how you were glad I'd moved heaven and earth to get here. It never crossed my mind that you'd be laying here on your deathbed being spoon-fed by this ignorant—"

"Who in the hell are you calling ignorant? You're the one who rolled up in here on some imaginary fairy tale only to get your face cracked!" Lori said as she shifted her weight from one foot to the other. I saw Lori scoop up some of my food with her fingers. I knew she was just waiting for the perfect time to fling it at Keysha. "You're lucky we're in this hospital room because if we were outside I'd deal with you. Right now I'm just going to ignore you and pretend you're not here."

Keysha placed the palm of her hand in Lori's face. "Talk to the hand, tramp!" Lori lost it. She stepped from behind Keysha's hand and slung the food, hitting Keysha on the side of her face. Keysha howled out like a mad woman and grabbed a handful of Lori's hair. Lori tired to reach up and pull Keysha's hair, but Keysha successfully avoided her.

"I will beat you down!" Keysha shouted as she tugged and yanked on Lori's hair.

"Let her go, Keysha!" I barked.

"This crazy whore doesn't know who she's messing with, Wesley! I will beat her down!"

"Keysha, please, let her go," I pleaded.

"Let me go!" Lori shouted as she continued to swing her arms.

"If you two don't stop, security is going to come in here and kick both of you out," I yelled. Keysha finally let her go, but Lori wasn't done just yet.

"Wait right there. I've got something for you!" Lori said as she rushed out of the room.

"Will you just chill for a second, Lori?" I said. But she was already gone. "Keysha, I'm glad that you came, but you didn't have to," I said, trying to calm her down.

Keysha was breathing very hard. "What do you mean, 'I didn't have to come'?" Keysha looked like she was emotionally on the brink. "Wesley, what are you saying?" She looked at me as if I were crushing her heart.

"Don't get me wrong, baby. I'm glad you're here, but I get the feeling that you being here has come at a bigger price than you can pay." I tried to be both sensitive and understanding, but it appeared as if every word that came out of my mouth was doing the exact opposite.

"You're in love with her now, aren't you?" I saw tears forming in Keysha's eyes.

"Keysha, it's not like that," I said.

"Yes it is, Wesley," Keysha stated with absolute conviction. She then brushed her fingertips across my forehead and then held them up before my eyes. Stuck to her fingers was the damning evidence that was causing

Keysha to act so uncharacteristically. Keysha had smeared Lori's lipstick off of my forehead. It was all too clear what Keysha had concluded.

"Her lipstick is all over your face and your lips! Don't even try to explain yourself, Wesley." Keysha's eyes were now spilling over with tears.

I had no idea how to respond or how to even begin to explain myself. I felt like a deer caught in headlights on a dark highway.

"I know how this might look to you," I said, finally finding my voice.

"Save it, Wesley." Keysha's voice trembled and cracked. "She's not prettier than me—her outfit is wack and she needs a good weave. So she must be keeping her legs open 24/7."

A nurse came in to see what all of the commotion was about. "Is there a problem in here? You guys are very loud and you're disturbing other patients who are trying to rest," she said.

"This is so stupid!" Keysha turned and walked away from me.

"Keysha, wait," I called out, but she refused to acknowledge me. She grabbed her suitcase, picking up a pair of socks that had fallen out, and hustled out of the room.

nine

KEYSHA

I rushed out of Wesley's room and down the hall to the elevator as quickly as I could. I didn't want him or that tramp to see me crying. I pressed the call button several times out of aggravation because I wasn't getting the instant service I needed. Finally, after what seemed like an eternity the elevator chimed. When the doors opened up I saw Wesley's dad getting off along with an elderly woman who I assumed was Wesley's grandmother.

"Keysha?" Wesley's father's voice was filled with surprise and confusion.

"Hello," I whispered quietly. I was so upset and didn't want to explain myself or what had just happened to me in Wesley's room.

"What are you doing here?" he asked as he exited the elevator. He held the door open for me as I stepped in.

"I don't know," I answered as tears streamed down my face.

"Are your parents here? Where are you going?" All I could do was shrug my shoulders and press the button for the lobby. He tried to keep the elevator door from closing but it was too late.

Once I reached the lobby, I exited the elevator and noticed a sign that read This Way to Chapel. I walked down a long corridor in the direction of the chapel. When I arrived I quietly entered the sanctuary and sat on a back-row pew. I was the only one in there, which suited me just fine. I sat heavily on the mahogany pew and pulled my legs up so my feet were resting on the bench. Hugging my knees, I let go of my emotions and sobbed in solitude.

I felt so stupid, dumb and humiliated. My heart ached so badly that it felt as if the pain was choking my soul to death. I hated myself for thinking that Wesley would be waiting for my arrival. My emotions were overwhelming and unmanageable. I didn't know if I'd ever bring myself to stop crying. I felt as if I'd been kicked in the gut by a mule. I hugged myself, rocking back and forth for a while, replaying how everything had just gone down. I then decided to lie down because I was exhausted and my head had begun to hurt. It wasn't long before I drifted off to sleep.

When I awoke I had a major cramp in my neck that I immediately tried to massage. I sat upright and stared at the wooden pulpit and the crucifix suspended high above it. I didn't know what I was going to do or where I was going to go. The only thing I was certain of was that I'd screwed up big-time. My unreasonable emotions and disrespectful mouth caused me to blindly toss away the best life that I could've ever hoped for, over a boy who was playing me for a fool. Numbness weighed down on me as the reality of my existence hit me hard like a punch from a prizefighter. Jordan probably didn't want to see me ever again, and I couldn't blame him for feeling that way. I had no place to go. I was low on cash and I longed for a hot shower. I placed my face in my hands and cried some more. I heard my phone vibrating. I opened up my purse, removed the phone and glanced at the caller ID. It was Maya.

"Hello," I answered tearfully.

"Oh, wow. You don't sound too good." Maya picked up on the sorrow in my voice right away. "What's going on, Keysha?"

"I've seen better days," I muttered, confirming her suspicions.

"Well, what happened? Did you make it there safely? Did you see Wesley? Is he okay? Is he paralyzed? Come on, Keysha, talk to me." Maya was eager to learn every detail.

"Maya, I've screwed up so badly," I said, sniffling.

"Keysha, what happened? You're scaring me," Maya admitted.

I took a few deep breaths and said, "My dad caught me at the bus station and gave me an ultimatum. He told me that if I came to see Wesley, I shouldn't bother coming back home."

"Damn. So you're still at home?" I could hear the disappointment in her voice.

"No," I answered. "I'm not at home."

"You mean you actually stood up against your dad

and went anyway?" Maya's voice rose to an earsplitting pitch.

"Yes," I admitted, realizing that I'd made a very foolish decision.

"It sounds as if you've found your true love. True passion makes you do extreme stuff like standing up to your parents. I read about this sort of stuff all of the time in my mother's old romance novels. You remind me so much of the characters in those books. Standing up to your father for the sake of your one true love." Maya was going off on some rose-colored fantasy.

"Well, it's too bad that my Prince Charming has eyes for another girl," I said, obliterating Maya's romantic pipe dream.

"Another girl?"

"Yes. Another girl. I think Wesley's the type of guy who likes to go around rescuing girls as if he's on some type of crusade to save every brokenhearted chickenhead he can find," I said earnestly.

"What kind of sense does that make? That doesn't even sound right, Keysha."

"Maya, there was another girl in the room spoon-feeding him. It was the girl he'd taken the bullet for."

"Well, did you beat her down?" Maya asked.

"I almost did, but I didn't have the strength because I was so hurt by his betrayal. I risked everything to be with him—I thought he loved me the same way that I loved him." I began crying once again. I couldn't help it. I was an emotional wreck.

"Don't cry, Keysha." Maya paused and listened as I

sobbed. "You're making me cry," she said, sniffling along with me. "What are you going to do now, Keysha? Do you think your dad will let you come back home?"

"I don't think so," I answered.

"I could talk to my mom and see if she'll let you crash here at my place for a few days until you can figure something out."

"Thanks, Maya," I said, wondering what it would be like staying at her place for a little while.

"What a jerk!" Maya said, now furious with Wesley. "How could he do that to you!"

"I don't know. All I know is that right now I want to leave this hospital, but I can't because I don't know where to go. I'm homeless, Maya. I am literally homeless."

"No, you're not. If my mom won't allow you to stay then I'll sneak you into my house." Maya wanted to make sure that I understood how far she'd go to support me during this difficult time.

"Thank you," I said as I exhaled while simultaneously smearing away my streaming tears. "Let me call you back. I need to find a bathroom so I can get myself together."

"Wait! How are you going to get back here?" Maya asked.

"I don't know, but I'll figure out something. I just need a little time alone to think things through."

"Promise me you'll call back."

"Yes, I promise to call you back," I said and ended the call. When I looked at my phone I noticed two things: the battery was very low and there were a number of calls from Jordan, Barbara and Wesley. Just as I was about to call Wesley back, I received an incoming call from Grandmother Katie. I really didn't want to talk to anyone from the family, but it was too difficult for me to ignore Grandmother Katie. I couldn't just tell her to go to hell and feel good about it.

"Hello," I answered in tears.

"Keysha?" Grandmother Katie's smooth voice was like a beautiful melody to my ears. However, I could hear the questions riding beneath her angelic voice.

"Yes," I whispered softly, almost afraid to speak. I knew that she must've been very disappointed and upset with me.

"Are you okay?" she asked.

"No," I said, leaning forward and glancing down at my feet.

"Are you in a safe place?" she asked.

"Yes."

"Do you need some help?" she asked, sensing I was in over my head. I was overjoyed to hear her offer me help after all the drama I'd caused. I thought for sure she'd phoned to disown me. I couldn't even bring myself to say yes because I was so choked up.

"Are you still there?" she asked.

"Jordan hates me now. I blew up at him and I can never go back there and—"

"Keysha, where are you?" Grandmother Katie asked in a firm but loving voice.

"At a hospital in Indianapolis sitting in the chapel going crazy," I answered.

"I want you to give me the name of the hospital and then I want you to sit tight until I arrive. Can you do that for me?"

"You're actually going to come here and get me?" I felt awful about her having to travel so far on my behalf.

"Well, you can't live in a hospital, honey. Besides, hospital food doesn't taste very good." I laughed a little at her comment.

"I have a little money left. I think I have enough to come to you," I said, offering her an alternative.

"No, that's not necessary. Let me come get you, baby. Now give me the address," she demanded.

"Okay," I answered and then gave her the information she requested.

When I ended my phone conversation with Grandmother Katie, I looked at all of the phone calls I'd gotten from Wesley. For a brief second I thought about returning his call, but then the image of him kissing Lori popped into my mind and upset me all over again. I then thought about calling Jordan and Barbara back, but I didn't know what to say. I didn't know how to explain myself and at that particular point I wasn't emotionally strong enough to deal with their disappointment. I decided to call Mike to see how things were going.

"Yo, this is your boy Big Mike. Leave a message and I might holla back." I didn't want to leave a message on his voice mail so I hung up the phone. I knew it would be a while before Grandmother Katie got there, so I decided to go look for something to eat. I walked out of the chapel and exited the hospital. I briefly wondered if Wesley's father would try to find me but hoped he wouldn't bother. I took a quick glance around and noticed a shopping center off in the distance.

"There's probably a McDonald's or something over there," I reasoned. When I arrived at the shopping center, I easily located the food court area. I ordered food from a Chinese restaurant and then found a place to sit and eat. After I ate, I walked around for a while and killed some time window-shopping. I was pleasantly surprised that the mall had a movie theater and decided to see what was playing. I had the option of watching several blockbuster films, but the one starring Will Smith won me over. After the movie ended, I walked back over to the hospital so that I could tell Wesley what else was on my mind. When I reached his room and walked inside, his bed had been made up as if he had never been a patient there. I went directly to the nurses' station.

"Excuse me, but can you tell me where Wesley Morris is?" I asked.

"Sure, hang on," said the nurse as she opened up a black binder and searched for his name. "Wesley Morris... Oh, yes, he was released earlier today."

"You mean he's gone?" I asked, wanting to make sure that I'd heard her correctly.

"Yes. He's gone home," the nurse repeated what she'd already told me. I exhaled a frustrated sigh.

"Are you okay?" she asked.

"Yes, I'm fine." I stepped away and pulled out my cell phone, but there was nothing I could do because the battery was dead. I knew for a fact that I'd forgotten my charger during my rush to leave the house.

"This entire situation is so lame," I muttered to myself as I headed back down to the chapel. When I reentered the sanctuary, I saw a priest dressed in black sitting next to an elderly woman. It was clear they were praying and I didn't want to disturb them. I took a seat in the last row and decided to lie down. I was so tired and mentally drained. I longed for the comfort of my bed, but that wasn't possible because of the foolish mistake I'd made.

I was jolted awake by someone shaking my shoulder and calling my name.

"Keysha," the voice said repeatedly.

"What?" I answered groggily as I sat upright. I had the worst cramp in my neck and my back ached.

"Come on. Let's go." I covered my eyes with my hand for a split second and then removed it. I squinted at Grandmother Katie, who looked as if she was exhausted from the long drive. The whites of her eyes were red and small pouches had formed below them. Bags beneath anyone's eyes was a clear indication of a restless night. She was dressed comfortably in blue jeans and an oversize sweatshirt that read I Love Jesus.

"Come on. We're going to go find a hotel room," she said, shaking me gently once more.

"Okay," I said and then gave her a giant hug. "I'm so happy to see you," I whispered to her.

"I know you are. Come on. We'll talk about all of this in the morning. Right now we both need to get some sleep." Grandmother Katie looked a bit weary but seemed happy to have found me safe and unharmed.

The following day I woke up to the sound of Grandmother Katie talking on the phone. I immediately knew that she was talking to someone about me. I decided to keep my eyes closed to keep up the appearance of being asleep. "Yes, she's with me now," I heard her say as she pulled back the drapes. "No, I just think she's a little confused and sorrowful right now.... Okay. We're going to go get something to eat and then head on back.... Okay, we'll see you then." Grandmother Katie then hung up the phone. I felt as if I wanted to sleep forever and never face a new day or the consequences that were waiting for me. I just wanted to drop off of the face of the earth and disappear.

Grandmother Katie moved around the small hotel room freshening up while humming a melody that filled the room with a special kind of enchantment. Eventually I just opened my eyes and stared at the ceiling.

"Well, good morning," Grandmother Katie said as she sat on the bed next to me and smiled as if we had agreed to take a road trip to Indianapolis together.

"Good morning," I replied as I hugged the pillow tightly against me.

Grandmother Katie lovingly stroked my shoulder and said, "I extended our checkout time until two o' clock this afternoon, but we only have one hour left. So I need you to get up, put on some fresh clothes so we can head on back home."

"Are you taking me back to your house?" I asked, not wanting to return home to face Jordan.

"Keysha, as much as I'd love for you to come stay with me, you have to get back home so you can be ready for school tomorrow morning."

"I don't want to go back home. I just want to crawl under a rock."

"I can imagine…however, you're still young and trust me when I say you're going to have days in your life that are going to feel one hundred times worse than this one." She gave me a reassuring smile.

"You're kidding, right? How can I possibly feel any worse than I do right now?" I asked. Grandmother chuckled.

"When you have children of your own, you'll understand. Now come on." She pulled back the bedding. "Let's get out and face the day standing upright with our heads held high."

"Okay," I said as I got out of the bed and entered the bathroom.

After Grandmother Katie and I ate lunch at a nearby Rainforest Cafe, we got on the highway and headed back toward Chicago. I fumbled with the radio in search of some good music to listen to. I wanted to hear some Lil Wayne, Jazmine Sullivan, or Fantasia.

"Right there, let that song play." Grandmother Katie had me stop at a gospel station. "That's Marvin Sapp," she said as she set the cruise control on her car.

"Marvin Sapp? I ain't never heard of no Marvin Sapp," I said, a little bit upset that I had to listen to her music.

"First of all, watch your grammar. Second, listen to what he's saying. He's saying he never would have made it, never could've made it, without you." Grandmother Katie began singing the lyrics. It was the first time I'd heard her sing and her voice was beautiful—robust and melodious and it had the power to give me goose bumps. Grandmother Katie sang the song with remarkable fervor.

She forced my ears to hear every word and suddenly, as if she'd cast some type of magical spell, I understood. I sang a verse with her even though I knew my voice was nowhere near as strong as hers.

Grandmother Katie encouraged me to keep singing along with her as best as I could, so I dutifully followed her lead. When the song ended, Grandmother Katie turned down the radio.

"You have a nice voice, Keysha. With a few voice lessons you'd probably sing like a bird," she said as she smiled at me.

"I had no idea you could sing like that. You should've gotten a recording contract with that voice. I'm for real. You're voice has a punch to it like Whitney Houston or Jennifer Hudson," I said, utterly amazed by the discovery of her voice. Grandmother Katie chuckled.

"When I was younger I'd thought about it. I used to stand in the bathroom mirror and pretend that I was Patti LaBelle all of the time and was supremely confident that I could give her a run for her money in a singing competition."

"Well, why didn't you become a singer?" I asked.

Grandmother Katie chuckled once again. "I used to be a part of a girl singing group called Sweet and Sexy when I was in college."

"Sweet and Sexy?" I laughed out loud because I could not imagine Grandmother Katie in a singing group called Sweet and Sexy.

"We were all sweet and naive church girls from different cities—Chicago, Oakland, Philadelphia, New York and New Orleans. We could harmonize and sing a cappella so beautifully. We were so amazing together that we could bring an audience to tears."

"Well, what happened? Did you guys ever get discovered?" I asked.

"No. We only stayed together for a semester. Two of the girls came up pregnant and the third one had to return home and help out her family, who fell on hard financial difficulties. I remained at school and joined the choir. I traveled around with the university choir all over the country, but after I got my degree and started working, singing sort of took a backseat. Well, at least any thoughts of a solo career did. I still sang with the church choir."

"Do you really think that I have a good voice?" I asked, feeling as if I'd discovered a new part of myself. I mean, I'd sung in the shower and in front of a mirror a million times, but I never thought my voice was worth hearing; and I certainly didn't realize that my own grandmother had such an amazing voice.

"Of course I do. A voice instructor has to determine your range and help you understand music."

"I've never thought about taking singing lessons. I think that's something I'd like to look into one of these days," I said.

"A lot of people learn how to sing in church," Grandmother Katie pointed out. "And church is a great place to learn."

"Okay, I get your hint. You want me to go to church more," I said, feeling as if the conversation was taking a different direction. "I probably need to stop at a church on the way back so that I can pray to God and ask him to allow Jordan to let me back in the house."

"You leave that part up to me." Grandmother Katie switched lanes to get around a slow-moving cement truck. "Now, tell me about this mess you've gotten yourself into."

I exhaled loudly. "I don't want to talk about it."

"Keysha…" Grandmother Katie insisted that I not shut down on her.

"I just screwed my entire life up. What more do you want to know?" I said sarcastically.

"Why did you disobey your father?" she asked.

"Because I felt he was being unreasonable. After all Wesley had done for me I felt that I needed to be with him."

"Honey, Wesley is not your husband. He's just a boy-friend and at this particular stage in your life chances are high that he's not going to be your last boyfriend."

"You can say that again," I uttered as I thought about the lipstick prints on Wesley's face.

"It sounds like your visit didn't go the way you'd planned." Grandmother Katie's intuition was correct as usual.

I didn't answer because I was trying to keep myself from crying about it.

"Wesley crushed your heart, didn't he? Did he tell you to go home?" Grandmother Katie asked.

"No." Once again I exhaled my frustration. "It just appears as if I'm not the only girl Wesley is dealing with. How could I have been so blind?" I whined.

"Don't blame yourself. When it comes to matters of the heart, things can get pretty complicated and confusing."

"Well, things between Wesley and me are definitely complicated," I admitted, feeling myself getting angry for risking so much just to be with him.

"Your relationship with your father has also reached a complicated level, wouldn't you say?"

"I know…you don't have to remind me. Do you think he'll let me back in? Or will my bags be packed and waiting for me at the door?" I asked, uncertain if I wanted to hear the answer to my questions.

"Of course he will. Let me tell you something about my son. He wants to give you a good home and a good life. He doesn't want to see you out on the streets. But you can't go around being hotheaded and disrespectful. That's not fair to him, Mike, or Barbara. Have you spoken to your father since you've been gone?"

"No, I haven't, but I did receive a number of messages from him and Barbara." I felt like a first-class jackass for what I'd done.

"They were very concerned and worried sick about you, Keysha. They called the police and filed a runaway report."

I dropped my jaw and held my mouth open. "They did what?" I couldn't believe what I'd just heard.

"They told the police you ran away from home and that if you were found by an officer, you were to be detained." Grandmother Katie drew her lips in a tight line, and I knew she wasn't joking around.

"They didn't have to do that."

"You didn't answer their repeated phone calls, Keysha, and they had no idea where you were. You're so lucky that you answered my phone call when you did. The police were about to do a phone trace on you to determine where you were. Then they were going to send a squad car for you. However, when you answered my phone call, I let Jordan know that you were okay and that I was on my way to pick you up."

"I'm sorry," I said as I began to cry.

"There's some Kleenex tissues in the glove compartment," Grandmother Katie said just as her cell phone rang.

"Hello," she answered her phone. "Yes, Jordan, she's with me now." She paused. "We should be there by dinnertime…. Okay, we'll see you then," she said and then hung up the phone.

"How mad is he?" I asked as I blew my nose.

"He isn't as angry as he is hurt. Jordan loves you, Keysha, and so do Barbara and Mike. I don't know what it's going to take for you to understand that, but I do know this—running away from a family who loves you unconditionally is a mistake that you can't afford to keep making."

"But I love Wesley, too," I said, trying to justify what I'd done. I thought for sure Grandmother Katie would understand my heart.

"I can understand that, but consider this—a young man will say that he loves you because he wants to win a prize such as sex. However, when a father says that he loves you, he's not looking for a prize. He truly means that he loves you and wants the best for you. That's the kind of man I raised and that's the kind of father you have in Jordan. Keysha, you don't realize how blessed you are. So many other men would've turned their back on you, but Jordan welcomed you."

"I know. I wasn't thinking...I just...I just felt that I needed to be with Wesley and when I got there I discovered that he didn't really need me the way I thought he did."

"You know, there is an old saying that goes something like this—'If you're going to walk on my love, the least you can do is take off your shoes.'"

"Interesting, I've never heard that saying before," I said, tilting my head slightly while pondering the meaning of the phrase.

"What do you think it means?" asked Grandmother Katie.

"Umm, I'm not exactly sure."

"It means not to take a person's kindness for granted. Stop taking this family's love for you for granted, Keysha. Are we clear on that?" Grandmother Katie was unmistakably serious and unyielding on her position.

"Yes." I fully understood that I was to never pull a stunt like this again.

ten

WESLEY

κeysha got me kicked out of the hospital after the fight she'd had with Lori. The nurse reported the incident and within an hour my doctor came by and gave me a quick examination, wrote a prescription and told me to follow up with an orthopedic doctor and dismissed me from the hospital. My dad, who wanted to know why Keysha was there and why she was so upset when he saw her getting on the elevator, grilled me once we got back to Grandmother Lorraine's house.

"Did something happen with that young lady that I should know about?" he asked.

"Dad, it's okay. I took care of it," I said, not wanting to give up any details about the fight. I sat down at the round walnut table in the kitchen.

"Took care of what, Wesley?" he asked, pressing the issue.

"Keysha just showed up unexpectedly, that's all." I tried to downplay her visit, but he wasn't buying it.

"Did you send for her, Wesley?" Dad asked, trying to get to the truth.

"No, I had no idea she was coming. I was happy to see her, but she got the impression that Lori and I were dating. She got a little upset over nothing," I explained. It was enough to give my dad a sense of what had gone down.

"Well, are you and Lori dating?" he asked.

"No," I answered. "She's just a friend."

"Okay." He seemed to accept my answers to his questions. "So where is Keysha now?"

"I don't know. I've called her a number of times, but she refuses to answer my calls," I said as I stood up and walked over to the cupboard. I opened it up and removed a box of microwave popcorn. I removed the plastic wrapping and placed the bag in the microwave. I set the timer for five minutes and then turned back toward my dad. I rested my behind against the countertop and tried to figure out a way to get in contact with Keysha.

"The police picked up that Percy kid," Dad said, changing the subject.

"Oh, yeah?" I responded, wanting to know more.

"Yup. They picked him up and formally charged him, but the police didn't find the gun he shot you with. The state prosecutor, a woman named..." My dad paused and pulled out his wallet. He removed a business card and read the name on it. "Amber Mullins says that they still have a good case, though, because Lori is testifying as an eye witness."

"Well, I'm glad Lori finally came around and agreed to help." I breathed a sigh of relief.

"Well, if she didn't come around on her own, I was certainly going to have a talk with her myself. Anyway, Attorney Mullins wants the judge to deny Percy bail because she feels he is a danger to himself and society. He goes before the judge in the morning. Hopefully, he'll be denied bail. However, if by chance he isn't, and he's able to make the bail payment, you and I are going to head down to the police station and file a restraining order against him."

"They should throw him under the jailhouse as far as I'm concerned," I said just as the kernels in the bag began popping. I removed the popcorn and skillfully opened the steaming bag before sitting back down at the table with my dad.

"You want some?" I offered.

"No, I'm not hungry."

"What's up with the rumor I heard about you and me staying in Indianapolis for good?" I wanted to know if Dad had a sudden change of plans without notifying me.

"Your grandmother has mentioned it to me a few times. She wants me to sell our home and move down here with her." He repositioned himself in his chair.

"You're not seriously considering it, are you?" I asked.

"No. The last thing I want to do is move back into the house with my mother. I love her, but moving back here is not a realistic option."

"Then I wonder why she told Keysha that—"

"Has your grandmother been going around spreading that lie?" Dad interrupted.

"Yeah, I think so." I scooped a handful of popcorn out of the bag.

"Well, I'll go talk to her and make myself very clear. How does your shoulder feel?" he asked, changing the subject.

"I'm okay, just a little achy right now."

"Well, Grandmother should be back any minute with your prescription."

"Good, because I can feel the pain medicine wearing off," I said, being honest about the discomfort I was feeling.

"I'll be sure to contact an orthopedist in the morning and schedule you an appointment," Dad said as he glanced out of the window. "Looks like your grandmother has just returned." He stood up to head toward the door.

"I'm going to go lie down for a little while." I picked up my popcorn bag and headed toward the basement.

I sat on the edge of my bed and finished eating. As soon as I was done, I called Keysha, but her phone went directly to voice mail. "Dang, girl, are you going to at least give me a chance to explain myself?" I spoke to her voice mail. "Give me a call back. Please," I requested before hanging up the phone.

I hated the way I felt. I felt as if I'd hurt her in such a way that she'd never want to speak to me again. Hurting Keysha was the furthest thing from my mind and I certainly wanted her to know and understand that. I let a few minutes go by and phoned her again, hoping that she'd pick up the phone. However, once more I was dumped into her voice mail where I left yet another message. Frustrated, I slipped off my shoes and rested on my back and glanced at the ceiling. I wondered why my life was in such a tailspin. Being shot was certainly no fun, and dealing with a girl as complex and unique as Lori was both challenging and exciting at the same time. Admittedly, I didn't know exactly how I felt about Lori and that left me in a strange state of confusion. I wasn't trying to be a player and see more than one girl at a time, but there was something about Lori that attracted me to her. I reached out and removed my iPod from the nightstand. Just as I was about to put the ear buds in my ears, I felt my cell phone vibrating.

"It's about time," I said aloud because I thought Keysha was finally returning my phone call. Without looking at the caller ID I picked up and answered.

"Hello."

"Do you miss me yet?" It was Lori. I had to give it to her; the girl was persistent.

"Did you make it home okay?" I asked.

"Yes, I'm here. Just washing my hair after being attacked by that pit bull you call a girlfriend. I swear, Wesley, you sure know how to pick 'em." Lori didn't have very high regard for Keysha. She continued her criticism. "She is all wrong for you. In fact you guys don't even look like a cute couple."

"I could say the same thing about you and Percy. You hooked up with a guy who is a little on the crazy side." I reminded her of her poor judgment call.

"Okay, point taken, but I honestly think that fate led us to each other," she said.

"Fate. How do you figure?" I asked as I rested one hand behind my head and got more comfortable.

"The way you rescued me from Percy was the first sign

that we belonged together. Then when you protected me from getting shot and killed was the second sign. Then when we kissed each other at the hospital. That kiss was so sweet I think destiny has brought us together. There is no denying it, Wesley. For some reason we're drawn to each other the way stars are drawn to the moon. Don't you agree?"

"I'm not too sure about all of that, Lori," I said, not fully accepting her theory of fate.

"You may not want to believe it and that's okay. But I do and I think that destiny will bring us together."

"I think that's kind of a long shot. You don't even like me that much," I reminded her.

"Well, my horoscope says that a new and very different love interest will enter my life and my relationship with this person will be both passionate and complicated." Lori summarized the astrology message she believed to be true for her.

"You don't believe me, do you?" she asked. "Well, here is more proof for you. According to your sign, you are torn between two lovers. However, your most recent love interest is more compatible and is perfect for you. You shouldn't hesitate and you should let your feelings be known. Now I know this may all sound a little on the bizarre side, but a lot of astrological stuff is true. I even heard that Missy Elliott consults the stars all of the time, and you know how successful she is. I'm telling you, Wesley. This stuff is powerful. So tell the truth and shame the devil. Were you thinking about me before I called?"

"Umm…" I said, not sure how to respond.

"See there. You need to stop fighting your feelings for me. You need to dump Keysha and give our relationship a chance." Lori was absolutely convinced that she and I belonged together and needed to hook up at all costs.

"Lori, just chill out for a minute, okay? You're talking a mile a minute," I complained. "There is so much going on. They've arrested Percy. We've got to testify in court and make sure that he's put behind bars for what he's done."

"I know. I've heard. I think that by going through this trial together, we'll become closer. Don't you think?" Lori asked.

"It's possible, but let's take one step at a time. The main thing right now is making sure that fool gets locked up," I said with a bit of anger in my voice.

"Okay. We'll take it one step at a time." Lori paused. "Do you want to come over and keep me company while I wash my hair?"

"No, my shoulder is still bothering me," I said.

"Oh, that was so insensitive of me. I'm sorry. I should come over to see you."

"No, don't do that. I'm about to take a nap," I said, preparing to end the call.

"You should let me take a nap with you," she teased.

"I'll talk to you later," I said, not wanting to exchange flirtatious comments with her.

A few days later when I returned to school it seemed as if everyone who saw me wanted to kick my ass just on GP…General Principle. Dudes I didn't even know glared at me, bumped into me and boldly called me a punk-ass snitch. The resentment and animosity toward me hung in the air like a cloud of black smoke from a burning inferno. For the first time in my life I actually feared for my own safety. I was defenseless and if some dude decided to swing a punch my way, I certainly had no way of properly defending myself. I tried to be as invisible as I possibly could, but no matter how hard I tried, I stood out because my arm was in a sling. I finally arrived at my locker and was having a difficult time opening it because I had to use my left hand. It took me a total of six tries before I got the lock opened. Then, suddenly some guy slammed the palm of his hand against the locker next to mine.

"You better watch your back!" said this dude, whom I didn't even know. He was slightly taller than me, had dark brown skin and a tattoo of a teardrop beneath one of his eyes.

"Look, man, I don't have a beef with you," I said, trying to defuse any aggression this dude had toward me.

"Percy is my cousin and if he gets locked up over some bogus lie about him shooting you, I'm going to dig a grave for you." Dude had a crazy, wild look in his eyes that made me believe every word he said. He slammed the palm of his hand against the locker once more and then walked away. I exhaled and tried to shake off the threat on my life. I reached for my English book and then closed my locker.

"These people are crazy, Wesley," Lori said as she approached my locker. "Two girls told me that they plan on beating me down as soon as the dismissal bell rings."

"Do you know them? Do you know their names?" I asked.

"Hell, no!" Lori was clearly upset.

"It's probably about Percy," I said.

"Duh! I know that much. I'm going to call my mom and tell her about this," Lori said. She glanced down the hallway in search of the two girls who were after her earlier. It was clear that she was a little paranoid.

"Yeah, that's probably a good idea. Maybe your grandmother can come pick you up."

"She's going to have to because I'm not about to get double-teamed by two girls. I didn't even do or say anything to these chicks." Lori and I stepped away from my locker.

"Don't let them scare you. They want you to be afraid of them, but you shouldn't be," I said.

"Too late because I am afraid of them. I told you, I'm the type of girl who likes to be protected from this sort of thing. And you only having one good arm isn't going to be enough."

"Gee, thanks," I said, feeling as if she'd just slapped me on the cheek.

"Don't take it personal, babes. It's not your fault. It is what it is. I'm just not going to get stomped over this mess with Percy."

"I feel you on that note. I just received a threat from Percy's cousin," I said.

"Who?" Lori asked.

"I don't know the guy's name." I shrugged my shoulders.

"What did he look like? Did he have a tattoo of a teardrop on his face?" she asked.

"Yeah, he did."

Lori raised an eyebrow. "You know the teardrop means that he's killed someone, right?"

"I know, but what I don't understand is why he isn't in jail for it, or at least in some type of reform school."

"I'm not sure if he's really killed anyone. And even if he did, who knows how everything went down? It may be a case where the police found a John Doe and haven't been able to solve the murder case," Lori explained.

"How do you know so much about that lifestyle?" I wanted to know if she was ever involved in some type of female gang.

"I know about it from a lot of places. The news, Percy, and even some of my own family members have gotten caught up in some mess. Anyway, the dude that threatened you is Percy's cousin, Claude. Percy and I hung out with Claude and his girlfriend on occasion and all I have to say is Claude is crazy. I'd stay away from him if I were you. Claude's a ticking time bomb."

"Trust me. I want nothing to do with the guy," I reiterated. "He seems like a really crazy dude."

"Crazy may be an understatement. Percy's dad is in jail and his mom is in rehab. Percy lives with his grandmother, who has one foot in her grave. Let's not talk about them anymore. I just want to focus on getting home without getting beat down. Do you want to get a ride with me? I know my grandmother won't mind."

"Cool. Meet me at my locker when the last bell rings," I said. Lori pulled me to the side and gave me a hug and planted a kiss on my cheek before turning down the hallway and heading to her class.

eleven

KEYSHA

It was 6:00 p.m. when Grandmother Katie and I pulled into the driveway. I was a nervous wreck and had no clue how severe my punishment would be. When Grandmother Katie turned off the engine I sat in my seat, afraid and frozen.

"Come on. You knew you had to face them at some point. You might as well go on in and get it over with so we can all move forward with our lives." Grandmother Katie wanted me to hold myself accountable for my actions.

"This isn't going to be pretty, is it?" I asked as I glanced over at her.

"What you did was unthinkable, but you're being given another chance. Remember what I told you about not taking this family's love for granted. Now get out and go on inside. I have to make a run to the pharmacy up the street."

"You mean you're not going to come in with me? I need your protection." I suddenly felt as if I were being thrown to a pack of wolves.

"It's not my place to interfere with or tell Jordan and Barbara how to raise you. I came to pick you up because I didn't want the police involved. I didn't want to see you locked up and placed back into the system and neither did Jordan or Barbara, but you left them with few options, Keysha."

"You're right," I said, accepting the difficult position I'd placed the family in. I opened the car door and got out. Grandmother Katie pulled off before I rang the doorbell. When Jordan came to the door he stepped aside and let me in.

"Hello," I greeted him politely. I avoided eye contact with him and looked at the ground.

"Are you okay?" I didn't expect him to ask that question. Jordan tilted my head up and gazed into my eyes.

"Yes," I answered.

"Step into my office. Barbara and I would like to discuss this with you," he said as he shut the door. I suddenly felt the urge to pee.

"Can I go to the bathroom first?" I asked.

"Yes," Jordan said.

I walked up the stairs and into the bathroom. Shortly thereafter, I walked into the basement and into Jordan's office. There were three chairs all facing each other. I sat down in the empty seat and remained silent.

"First of all, how is Wesley doing?" Barbara asked.

"I think he's going to be fine. He was able to sit up and talk," I said as I repositioned myself in the seat.

"Where was he shot?" Jordan asked.

"In the shoulder," I answered.

"So he's going to pull through, right?" Barbara asked as she leaned forward and rested her elbows on her thighs.

"Yes," I answered with a trembling voice.

"Good," Barbara stated before repositioning herself in her chair.

Jordan jumped right in and let his feelings be known. "This entire incident has left a very sour taste in my mouth, Keysha. You disobeyed me, you fought me and you ran away from me. I called the police and made plans for you to be placed into a mental hospital."

"A mental hospital?" I glanced into his eyes to see if he was for real.

"Yes. I wanted you to be detained pending a psychiatric evaluation."

"But I'm not crazy." I wanted to make that very clear.

"Keysha, you did a one-hundred-eighty-degree turn on me when I found you at the bus station. You were acting like a totally different person." For the first time I was seeing myself through Jordan's eyes.

"I thought I was doing the right thing." I tried to get them to understand the incident from my perspective.

"By boldly defying us?" Barbara asked.

"I didn't mean to rebel or fight back the way I did. I'm sorry for what I did."

"I don't know. I still think we should get you some professional help. I know of a place that deals with teenagers in need of mental therapy." Jordan wasn't convinced that my outburst was an isolated incident.

"You guys can't be serious," I countered, feeling as if they were just joking around.

"Oh, no, we're very serious, Keysha." Barbara gave me a look that sent a chill down my spine. I knew she wasn't playing around.

"I'm sorry. I really am. I won't do it again. Trust me. After what I went through with Wesley, I've certainly learned my lesson. You can punish me or do whatever, but please don't ship me off to some mental hospital!," I said, apologizing for what I'd done.

"Does your mom have a history of mental illness, Keysha?" Barbara asked.

"I don't know," I said.

"Did she seem to have two personalities?" Jordan asked.

"Of course she did. Justine is as crazy as—" I caught myself and stopped speaking.

"It could be a genetic thing," Jordan said to Barbara, who seemed to be agreeing with him.

"You guys are freaking me out here. Yes, my mother is crazy, but she's always been that way. I'm nothing like her. I'm not mentally challenged in any way." I once again tried to reassure them of my sanity.

"How can we be sure, Keysha? What assurances do we have that you won't have another outburst and do something like this again?" asked Barbara, who looked me directly in the eyes.

"I promise you." I started tearing up. For the first time I realized the severity of what I'd done. "I will never, ever pull a stunt like that again. I will be respectful and do as I'm told. Please do not ship me off to some nuthouse where they'll strap me down to a table and leave me locked up in a padded room." Jordan and Barbara looked at each other briefly, as if they were making some type of silent determination.

"Keysha, go up to your bedroom," Jordan said. I didn't say anything as I stood and exited the room. Jordan closed the door behind me, so I couldn't hear what he and Barbara were talking about.

I walked into my bedroom and crash-landed facedown on my bed. I rested for twenty minutes before getting back up to turn on my computer. As my computer was booting up, Mike entered.

"How did it go?" he asked as he sat down on my bed. "How much trouble are you in?"

"Oh, I'm in some pretty deep water. They're talking about shipping me off to a mental institution. Have they ever threatened to send you to the nuthouse?" I asked Mike.

"No, never. That's pretty deep, though," Mike said, feeling empathy for me.

"How are things going for you?" I asked, wanting to know if Jordan had forgiven him yet for wrecking his car.

"About the same. I wish I could turn back the hands of time and undo all of the stuff I've done, but I can't. By the way, how is Wesley doing?" Mike asked.

"*Please.* Don't even mention his name to me," I said, not wanting to deal with the memory of what I saw at the hospital.

"That bad, eh?" Mike asked.

"You have no idea. How is your girlfriend, Sabrina?"

"She's cool. I've talked to her a few times. She wants to hook up once I come off of being grounded."

"How long will you be tied down for?" I asked.

"Don't know. Jordan didn't give me a set amount of time. At this point, it is what it is," Mike said, shrugging his shoulders.

"Grandmother Katie should be back soon," I informed him as I kicked off my shoes.

"Cool, I'm going down to the spare bedroom and get some of my stuff out of there. She's probably going to stay for the night."

"Yeah she is," I confirmed. Mike exited my bedroom and walked down the hall. Once my computer was up, I typed in www.myspace.com/keyshasdrama and checked to see if I'd gotten any e-mails or hits to my page. As soon as I logged in I got an instant message from Maya via Skype.

Maya: Where u been?

Keysha: It's a long story.

Maya: I sent u a bazillion txt mgs. Y U ain't answer me?

Keysha: Fone is dead. Need 2 recharge it.

Maya: Who's computer r u on?

Keysha: Mine. I'm @ home now.

Maya: When u get back?

Keysha: Not 2 long ago.

Maya: They let u back in da house?

Keysha: Yeah, but they talkin' bout puttin' me in a mental hospital.

Maya: Mental hospital! R U serious?

Keysha: Yeah. They think I got a split personality or somethin'.

Maya: Damn.

Keysha: I no. Try n 2 let them no I ain't crazy like that.

Maya: How u get back home so quick?

Keysha: Grandmother came & got me.

Maya: So u think yo folks really gonna ship u off 2 da funny farm?

Keysha: I hope not. Will keep u posted though.

Maya: K.

Keysha: How u been? N E thing new going on?

Maya: Did I tell u I went to planned parenthood?

Keysha: What? When u do that and what 4?

Maya: 2 get some birth control pills. Thinking bout doing it with Misalo.

Keysha: 4 real?

Maya: Yeah I think I'm ready 4 it.

Keysha: Girl u need 2 b real sure b-cause dudes will start acting funny on u once they get it.

Maya: Misalo is not like that. He loves me. We R so into each other. It's hard 2 put in 2 words. All I no is our romance needs 2 b made into a movie b-cause it is so strong.

Keysha: Huh, that's the way I used 2 feel about Wesley until I walked in on him and saw lipstick all over his face.

Maya: Well Misalo is not like Wesley. He would never do something stupid like that b-cause he knows I would go totally loco on his azz.

Keysha: Say what u want 2 but my love is on lockdown.

Maya: Well, my love is open and ready 4 business. But when u get off of da love lock down thing, let me no b-cause I no where u can get some birth control pills w/o a lot of drama.

Keysha: Where at?

Maya: Planned Parenthood. Same place where I got mine.

Keysha: Nope. I am kool 4 now but I hope u no what u r doing.

Maya: Don't hate!

Keysha: I ain't hatin' on u. I'm just sayin' make sure he don't get it & then start acting all stupid.

Maya: Misalo isn't stupid.

Keysha: Neither was Wesley until Lori came along.

Maya: Stop comparing Misalo to Wesley. U pissin' me off with dat.

Keysha: Sorry. Just tryin' to b a good friend.

Maya: Then just b supportive.

Keysha: OK.

Maya: U coming to school in the morning?

Keysha: Yes.

Maya: Tryouts for the school play is this week. There R A lot of open slots. U should consider reading 4 a part.

Keysha: I will think about it. G2G. I hear people coming. TTYL.

I arrived at school early the next morning, so I could stop in the cafeteria, grab a doughnut and catch up with Maya. I'd just sat down when Maya showed up and slammed her books down on the table.

"Watch my stuff for me while I grab something to eat," she said as she stepped away. She had on a pink-and-blue Rocawear hoodie with a blue jean skirt and white All Star gym shoes. Her outfit was cute. When Maya returned she sat down across the table from me.

"I swear some of the kids at this school are just too ignorant for words," Maya complained.

"What's wrong?" I inquired as I bit into my doughnut.

"Nothing, I just overheard some guys who were standing in line talking about how they planned to fight some other kids after school over at Mr. Subs. That is so stupid. Why would you go to a restaurant just to fight?"

"I don't know. When I get into it, I just fight. I don't pick a venue first," I answered honestly.

"Well, that's different. I mean if you're defending yourself or something like that then it's cool," Maya huffed. "So what happened with your folks? How much trouble are you in?"

"God, we had this long drawn-out discussion last night once I got off the computer with you. They're sending me to a psychiatrist for an evaluation to make sure I'm adjusting well and that I don't have some hidden personality or some crap like that."

"Damn! They aren't playing, are they?" Maya was without a doubt surprised by my parents' decision to schedule a session with a headshrinker.

"I really don't want to go, but what other choice do I have?"

"Maybe it will be helpful," Maya suggested.

"I don't see how. I'm not crazy—at least I don't think that I am."

"You're not crazy, well, at least not psychopathically insane." Maya's observations weren't helping me to feel any better.

"After some fussing I agreed to go as long as I was just being evaluated," I said.

"So when do you go?" Maya inquired.

"Barbara is calling today to schedule an appointment," I said, dreading the entire idea.

"Did you get grounded, too?" Maya asked.

"Yeah, I'm on lockdown for a while. I can't go to parties or anything. I have to come home directly after school and all that jazz."

"Dang. I really wanted you to try out for the play." Maya sounded disappointed.

"Maya, I've never done anything like that before. I'd probably suck at it." I immediately shot down the idea.

"I think you'd be great. With a little help and some practice, I'm positive you'd be able to sharpen up your already awesome acting skills. You're really a natural, at least in my opinion you are."

"Is there any singing involved?" I was mildly curious.

"Yes, there is, but not very much and we sing as a group, primarily."

"My grandmother told me I had a nice singing voice," I confided.

"Really?" Maya answered, amazed by this news.

"Yes. When we were driving home we were singing in the car together. She believes that with some coaching I could do well."

"See, that's all the more reason you need to try out. The choir director is helping out with the play and you could pick up a few pointers if you make it." Maya wasn't willing to let me accept defeat without trying.

"Do you really think I have a chance?" I asked, uncertain of my ability.

"Of course I do. Look, as long as you know how to read and not stumble over your lines you'll make it. Besides, I'll help you," Maya said.

"Well, let me ask if it's okay. If I get permission, I'll let you know and then we could set up some time to practice."

"Really work on getting your folks to say yes. I want you to be a part of the drama club." Maya glanced at the clock on the wall. "I've got to run. I need to catch up with Misalo before class begins. You know how it is when you need a kiss before you go to class." Maya was smiling from ear to ear as she gathered up her belongings and rushed off.

I came directly home after school like I was instructed. Once I got in the house, I called Jordan to let him know that I'd arrived safely.

"Is Mike in the house with you?" Jordan asked.

"Yes. He went out to the garage to get a ladder so he could change a lightbulb in his room," I informed him.

"Okay, I should be home in a little while. Grandmother Katie left earlier today. She said she'd call you later on this evening. We've also scheduled an appointment for an evaluation." Jordan was being very direct and to the point. I cringed at the thought of being evaluated. I didn't feel like opening up to some stranger who knew nothing about me.

"Dad, can I ask you a question?" My voice trembled with nervousness.

"Yes?"

"You think it would be okay for me to try out for the school play? I realize that I'm springing this on you at the

last minute, but I think it's something I'd really like to try."
I pulled the phone away from my ear in anticipation of a
loud and negative response.

"School play?" I could hear the additional questions
floating beneath his inquiry.

"Yes. I think I'd like to try out for a role. I've never been
a part of one or done anything like it before and I want
to try out. I realize I'm grounded and need to get evaluated and all, but tryouts are only for one day. So I'm
asking for permission to stay after school on the day of
tryouts to see if I have what it takes to be a part of the
drama club." There was dead silence. After what seemed
like an eternity Jordan finally spoke.

"Let me think about it, Keysha." Jordan was reluctant
to give an answer. However, I took his response as a
positive sign.

When Barbara and I arrived at the office of Dr. Pat Ursa
I was nervous and uncomfortable. My palms were sweaty,
my heart was racing and I felt nauseous. As we sat in the
waiting room, I glanced around at other patients, searching for any behavior that would indicate someone was
criminally insane. I thought for sure I'd see some murderer
or some nutcase who liked talking to imaginary people
inside of walls or something. But I didn't see anyone who
fell into that category. There was a middle-aged woman,
who on the surface appeared completely normal. She
picked up a copy of *Family Circle Magazine* and began
thumbing through it. There was another guy dressed in a
very nice suit fumbling around with his BlackBerry.

"This is nothing like I imagined it would be," I whispered to Barbara, who'd just sat down next to me after filling out some paperwork with the receptionist.

"What did you think it would be like?" Barbara asked as she stuffed her wallet back down into her purse.

"Full of crazy people wearing straitjackets, sitting in white padded rooms banging their heads against the wall."

"We're not in a mental institution, Keysha." Barbara took my hand into her own and began rubbing it. Her touch was soothing.

"I'm sorry about all of this." I spoke from my heart. "I mean—I don't know what I mean. I just don't want to say the wrong thing and end up on some operating table getting my head shaved in preparation for brain surgery."

"Keysha, you're letting your imagination get the best of you," Barbara said as her cell phone began to vibrate. She answered it and I could tell it was Jordan. After she informed him of our location she handed the phone to me.

"Hello," I said.

"Just relax, Keysha. It will be okay. It's not uncommon for people to see a psychiatrist."

"Have you ever seen one?" I boldly asked.

"Yes." Jordan's answer surprised me.

"What for?" I inquired.

"Grief counseling. After my dad passed away I had some trouble adjusting to the loss. Dr. Ursa helped me through that difficult time."

"Oh. I see," I responded, not certain of what to say next.

"We'll talk more when you get home," he said before asking me to let him speak to Barbara once again.

I went in to see Dr. Ursa, who was a man with steely gray-and-black hair. He had deep-set and warm eyes, slightly bushy eyebrows and an oversize forehead. He appeared to be in his mid-fifties and in great shape for his age. He asked me to have a seat in a chair situated in front of his desk. I sat down and began to scan the room, feeling a little weird and slightly paranoid.

"Are you comfortable?" he asked, seemingly concerned about my well-being.

"I'm cool," I answered as I looked at his degrees displayed on the wall.

"How do you feel today?" he asked.

"Crazy—I mean not crazy in the traditional sense of crazy. I mean…never mind."

"It's okay to feel a little strange or out of place. A lot of my patients feel the way you do when they first come to my office. However, in due time you'll probably look forward to your visits."

"Oh. I won't be coming back, that's for sure. You need to ask me some questions, right?" I wanted to get right to the heart of the matter so that I could move on with my life.

"No. I don't want to ask you anything. I'd prefer to talk about whatever is on your mind." I didn't expect Dr. Ursa to say that. I also didn't expect for him to be so calm and easygoing.

"Well. How long have you been a doctor?" I was curious.

"Well over twenty years," he answered.

"Why did you want to become a psychiatrist?"

"I didn't want to be a doctor at first. I wanted to be a jazz singer, but I just didn't have the voice for it."

"I cannot imagine you singing jazz." I chuckled. "Now my Grandmother Katie, she could've been a jazz singer. She has a beautiful voice."

"It sounds like you're close to Grandmother Katie," Dr. Ursa ventured.

"I like her a lot. But we really haven't known each other for very long."

"Is that so?"

"Yeah. She and I got off to a great start when we met. Have you ever met someone and the two of you instantly hit it off?" I asked.

"Yes," he answered.

"Well, that's how it was with Grandmother Katie and me. Felt like I'd known her for years and I've been acquainted with her for less than a year."

"It sounds as if she's a very special woman." Dr. Ursa got that one correct. He and I continued to make small talk about school, my friends and my mother, whom I really didn't want to talk about on any level.

"Do you not like your mother?" Dr. Ursa struck a sensitive nerve with that question.

"I don't want to talk about her at all. So just drop it, okay?" I scowled. I suppose the expression that formed on my face was a rather nasty one, which Dr. Ursa took note of. My mother was a very selfish woman and cared only about herself. When I lived with her, she put us in a lot of dangerous situations. My mother's biggest problem was she loved the criminal lifestyle. She was allergic to holding down a good ol' nine-to-five job and the consequences of a jail sentence didn't deter her.

"It's okay. We don't have to talk about her." He finally agreed to drop the topic of my mother. Discussing my mother was the only taboo subject that caused an immediate emotional knee-jerk reaction during the course of our meeting. Once we got past that wrinkle in the road, I put forth a yeoman's effort to demonstrate how normal I was. After all, I wasn't suffering from peculiar obsessive behavior like walking around in circles for no reason, or standing in a corner licking wallpaper. Nor did I walk around having detailed conversations with invisible friends who accompanied me.

Dr. Ursa talked with Barbara and Jordan via telephone afterward. Dr. Ursa informed them that he wanted to schedule more sessions with me. The agitation of having to sit through therapy when there was absolutely nothing ailing me was beyond comprehension. Dr. Ursa believed I had some unresolved anxiety and abandonment issues with my mother, which caused periodic erratic emotional behavior. That was a bunch of bull because I really didn't care about my mother or anything she did. I totally didn't even think about her and under no circumstances did I ever want to see her again. I mean, what was wrong with that? For example, if some burglar breaks into your home and kills your family, would you want to have dinner and a conversation with the guy? Probably not! My mother was the type of woman who could cause chaos at a one-man parade. She'd find some way to trip the guy just for the hell of it. She was just not the type of person I wanted to be around. Personally, I believed Dr. Ursa was looking forward to generating an enormous bill to submit to

Jordan's insurance company, but of course I couldn't prove my theory. By the time my parents and Dr. Ursa had reached an agreement, I had no choice but to attend future sessions—something I wasn't looking forward to.

Jordan and Barbara agreed to allow me to try out for the school play, which was called *Teenage Love Affair*. Just as Maya had promised, she coached me for the audition. On the day of tryouts I was very nervous, but Maya encouraged me and insisted that I just relax and let everything come naturally. When it was my turn to read, I walked into the school auditorium and onto the stage. I stood in front of the play directors and stated my name. I exhaled a few times then acted out the lines I'd memorized. When I was finished I exited the stage and met up with Maya in the hallway outside the school auditorium.

"You did good," Maya said, smiling at me.

"No. I don't think so, Maya. I was so nervous. I was shaking like a wet cat stuck in the middle of a blizzard," I admitted.

"You did just fine. Your voice is so unique and strong. I'm positive you'll get picked for one of the parts."

"Ha, that's a laugh. There is no way a rookie like her is going to make the cut," said this girl who was eavesdropping on our conversation. She was about my height and had long hair that cascaded down to her shoulders. She was a little on the thick side and had on too much lip gloss because her lips looked as if she'd just finished eating a bucket of chicken. She combed her fingers through her hair as if to say, "I have long hair and you don't."

"Priscilla, no one was talking to you, so why don't you just see your way out of our conversation." Maya quickly put her in check.

"Hey, I'm just telling the girl the truth instead of filling her head with false hope. Girlfriend, you can't act," Priscilla said directly to me. I couldn't believe this chick just appeared out of nowhere and offered up a nasty attitude instead of friendship and encouragement. I sized up Priscilla. She was a big-boned girl, rather tall with fish eyes and a gap between her upper front teeth. Enormous boobs, and full baby-mama hips.

"Keysha, don't pay her any attention. Priscilla Grisby is just afraid of competition. You and her both tried out for the same part."

"And I know for a fact that I'm going to get the part," Priscilla said, boldly proclaiming her victory.

"The only reason you want the part is so you can be all up in Antonio's face. He doesn't want you, Priscilla." Maya was clearly becoming irritated.

"All the boys want me. Including your boyfriend, Misalo. I could have him just like that!" Priscilla popped her fingers. "If I wanted him."

"Oh, hell no. Keysha, hold my coat." Maya was getting ready to fight. She removed her earrings, unlatched her necklace and spit out her the gum she was chewing. I pulled her away before any hair was pulled or any skin was clawed.

"Come on, girl. Let's go before this gets out of hand," I said as I moved her away from the explosive situation.

"Ooh, I can't stand that girl!" Maya railed. "She just makes my skin crawl."

"She's probably right, though. I didn't think I was all that good, Maya."

"Keysha, you were much better than her. She uses her looks to get her way. She's just a spoiled brat who's used to getting her way. She *sucks* as an actress! You've got more natural talent in your big toenail than she'll ever have."

I laughed.

"I'm serious, Keysha." Maya began laughing with me.

"Come on, girl. I've got to get to my locker so I can get my stuff. I've got a ton of homework that needs to get done."

twelve

WESLEY

AS my court day drew closer, so did the unwanted visits from Claude and a few other goons, whose sole purpose was to intimidate and antagonize me. I decided to try to handle this on my own without getting my dad involved, because he was already dealing with construction workers who were repairing our house, as well as medical issues he was having from the burns he suffered when our house caught fire. I didn't want to burden him with any more drama than I already had. I decided to report Claude to the principal, who called us both down to the office to have a discussion and to squash the beef between us. I arrived at the principal's office first. The principal, Mr. Dewey, looked fairly young, about twenty-eight years old. He had light brown skin the color of corn muffins, cascading dreadlocks and was fond of wearing bow ties.

"How is your shoulder coming along, Wesley?" he asked as I sat in a seat in front of his desk.

"It's okay. Just sore and stiff," I answered.

"How long will your arm be in a sling?" he asked.

"The orthopedist says anywhere from ten to twelve weeks. Then I go in for physical therapy," I said. There was a knock at his door and I looked over my right shoulder and saw Claude standing in the doorway.

"I got a message saying you wanted to see me," Claude stated as if he were completely annoyed by the fact he was called into the office.

"Yeah, Claude, have a seat," said Principal Dewey. Claude sat down in the empty seat next to me. "I believe you already know Wesley Morris," said Mr. Dewey as he took a seat behind his desk.

"Nope, I don't know him at all," Claude lied as he slouched down in his seat. He fully extended his right leg, then placed his right hand on his crotch while simultaneously digging in his ear with his left index finger.

"That's a lie," I said, exasperated.

Claude glanced over at me and once again said, "I've never seen you before." He removed his finger from his ear and flicked the brown, sticky earwax on his finger in my direction. I instinctively moved out of the way so his ear slug wouldn't land on me.

Mr. Dewey got to the heart of the matter. "Wesley says that you've been harassing him. Is that statement accurate?"

"I don't know what he's talking about." Claude stuck to his lie.

"Claude, you know you're skating on thin ice. You've been involved in a number of altercations this year and if you get involved in one more, off to reform school you go. And I can guarantee you they are not going to put up with your macho attitude."

"Macho? What in the world does that mean?" Claude asked, looking perplexed.

"He means that no one is going to put up with your bull," I explained to him in a condescending tone as if he were dumb for not knowing the meaning of the word. Claude's eyes were suddenly ablaze with hate. That's when I knew I'd just made things worse.

"Claude, if I even so much as hear that you've bumped into Wesley, I'm kicking you out of this school. And Wesley…"

"Yes, sir," I answered Mr. Dewey.

"Stay away from him and don't aggravate or taunt him in an effort to get him to mess up."

"Trust me. I don't want anything to do with him," I assured him. "He's all ticked off at me because his cousin is in jail for trying to kill me." Mr. Dewey leaned back in his seat and remained quiet. His eyes darted back and forth from me to Claude.

"All of this violence among young people has got to come to an end. It seems to me as if your generation is hooked on violence like it's some sort of narcotic. Claude, is your locker near Wesley's?" asked Mr. Dewey.

"I don't know," answered Claude.

"Boy, stop lying. Your last name is Morgan and Wesley's last name is Morris, so I'm pretty sure your locker is near his." Mr. Dewey removed a sheet of paper from his top desk drawer.

"Claude, I'm going to assign you a new locker on the

other side of the school so you won't be tempted to do something stupid. I'm going to save you from yourself. Wesley, is he in any of your classes?"

"No, sir," I replied.

"Good. The less you two see of each other the better."

"I like my locker where it is. Make him move to the other side of the school," Claude complained.

"No, Claude. Effective immediately, I'm assigning you a new locker," Mr. Dewey said unapologetically. "Wesley, you're free to go. Claude, you wait right here while I fill out this locker transfer form and escort you to your current locker so that you can gather your belongings."

"Thank you," I said as I rose to my feet and hastily exited Mr. Dewey's office.

"Wesley," the principal called. I stopped and turned. "Don't forget to pick up a hall pass at the front desk."

"Okay," I said, feeling very relieved.

When the dismissal bell rang, I waited by the gymnasium doors for Lori, who'd sent me a text message earlier telling me that she'd be taking the school bus back home with me. When I saw her coming down the hall, I smiled. She was wearing tight blue jeans, a green top and sexy high-heeled leather boots. It was obvious she was supremely confident and comfortable strutting in them by the seductive manner in which her hips swiveled. As other male students passed her by, they turned around to gaze at her behind. I glanced at her with a mannish smile, glad she was coming to meet up with me. Then in the back of my mind, images formed of us embracing in each others' arms and kissing. I allowed myself to enjoy all of the intimate possibilities that could happen between us.

"Hey, handsome," Lori greeted me with a hug and a kiss on the cheek.

"What's up?" I said as I led her out the door and toward the school buses.

"The usual stuff. Fighting with my mom and grand-mother. They're so damn old-fashioned. It's annoying at times," Lori complained. "How are things going with you?"

"Okay, considering." I sighed.

"That doesn't sound too good, Wesley." Lori heard the uncertainty in my voice.

"Everything is fine. I just had a little problem, which I've taken care of."

"Good, because I like a strong man who knows how to take care of business," Lori answered, flirting with me.

"Well, I'm the type of guy who likes to use my head to solve problems and not my fists," I proudly proclaimed as we stepped onto the school bus and took a seat.

Later that evening, I found myself sitting at the kitchen table working on my math homework. Grandmother Lorraine was at church making food baskets for women in a local homeless shelter. Dad was in his room looking over some documents regarding his long-term disability payments. I was about to work through my last algebraic equation when a phone call from Lori came through. I was going to ignore her, but decided to answer at the last minute.

"Took you long enough," Lori whined.

"I'm busy doing my homework," I said, feeling as if I really didn't have to explain anything to her.

"Well, it's time for you to take a break and talk to me." Lori was being bossy.

"Says who?"

"Me," Lori said. "So I was thinking that we should—" At that very moment another call was coming through. I glanced at the caller ID. Keysha's name lit up the display.

"Finally," I uttered.

"What do you mean, 'finally'?" Lori was confused by my comment.

"Lori, I've got to go. I'll holler at you later." Before she could say anything further, I clicked over to Keysha.

"Hello," I answered frantically.

"Hello, Wesley," Keysha greeted me.

"I've missed you so much. Do you know that?"

"Yeah, right. You're not missing me one bit."

"Yes, I am. Believe me, I miss you an awful lot," I insisted, stating my case.

"So, do you have something to say to me? You've been calling me like a deranged stalker."

"That's because I'm in love with you and my heart was broken when you didn't return my calls."

"Wesley, your heart is nowhere near broken. Last time we were together you seemed to be getting along just fine. And you know what really ticks me off with you, Wesley?"

"No."

"The fact that you gave me the impression that things were so difficult for you there. You had me thinking that every day you were alive was a blessing. How could things be so dangerous? Yet you found time to kick off a new romance. What in the hell is that about?"

"Keysha, you don't understand. It's not—"

"Wesley!" I heard my father scream out my name. He then came running into the kitchen with a wild and panicked look in his eyes.

"What's going on?" I asked, immediately sensing something was way off base. He opened up a nearby closet door and removed one of several baseball bats Grandmother Lorraine kept hidden around the house in case an intruder got in.

"Call the police!"

"The police?" I was suddenly confused by his request.

"Don't you hear my car alarm going off? How could you have not heard glass shattering?" he barked as he rushed out into the night.

"Keysha, I'll call you back!" I hung up on her before she could say another word. I phoned the police and gave them the address. They said a squad car would be there within a few minutes. I then rushed out the door to catch up with my father. Sure enough someone had vandalized his car.

"Look at this." Dad was at his wit's end. Someone had poured yellow and green paint all over his car, then smashed out the passenger's and driver's side windows. "Oh, this is the last thing I need right now."

"I'm going to go find out who did this," I said as I started running down the street as best as I could with one arm in a sling.

"Wesley, get back here!" My father chased me down. Once he caught me, he walked me back toward the house. "You don't need to go chasing someone like a lunatic. The police will come and we'll make a report to the insurance company."

"Why does everyone in this crazy town hate us? We haven't done anything to anyone!" I was furious and wanted retribution.

My father placed his hands on my shoulders and looked directly into my eyes. "Wesley, calm down. It's just a car and it can be replaced." My father was surprisingly composed about the situation.

"It's not right." I began pacing.

"I know it isn't right, but we'll get through this. Why don't you go look in the garage and see if you can find some old rags that we can get some of the paint off with?"

"What if they come back?" I asked, wanting to protect my father.

"Don't worry about that. I'm sure the police will be along any moment now." As I walked back toward the garage I heard a rapid popping sound off in the distance. It sounded as if someone had lit a string of firecrackers. I entered the garage and flipped the light switch. I looked around and found an aged wooden trunk filled with old clothes. I grabbed a handful and walked back toward the front of the house where my Dad's car was parked. Just as I returned, a squad car was approaching. Dad walked out into the street to flag down the police. I dropped the clothes on the ground near the car and shook my head with disgust. As two police officers walked over to take a look at my dad's vandalized car, I received a phone call. I removed my phone and saw that Lori was calling me.

"Hello," I answered with an angry tone.

"Wesley, this is crazy!" Lori was hysterical.

"Lori, are you okay?"

"No, I'm not. The police are on the way over here."

"The police? What in the hell is going on?"

"Someone just drove by and opened fire on our house!"

thirteen

KEYSHA

"Maya, you won't believe what just happened." I had called her up when Wesley hung up the phone on me.

"What? I'm all ears."

"That fool Wesley hung up the phone on me." I was totally ticked off.

"No, he didn't. Stop lying on him, Keysha."

"Girl, I am not lying. I was pouring my soul out to him by letting it be known how crappy I felt after my hospital visit and how I didn't appreciate his little love affair on the side. Then out of nowhere he cut me off and said, 'I'll call you back later.'"

"I'll bet that tramp was there with him," Maya said.

"I think you're right. He probably didn't want her to know that he was on the phone with me," I concluded.

"Did you call him back?"

"Hell, no. Keysha Kendall does not chase down men.

If he wants to be with her stanky ass then so be it. I don't want to be with a guy who doesn't want me."

"Why do you think he's suddenly trying to be a player?" Maya asked.

"She's probably sexing him to death and now he suddenly can't think straight. I'm telling you, Maya, when I walked into his hospital room he looked at me as if he was about to have a coronary. I swear his eyes got really big and he looked like he'd just gotten caught watching Internet porn or something."

"And he had lipstick all over his face, right?" Maya wanted to be certain.

"He had lipstick everywhere. Hell, it looked like he'd had a lipstick party in his room."

"You know what? That's just a cut-and-dried case of cheating."

"I can't believe he's doing this to me! Why is he being such a jerk?" I wanted to cry, but I held on to my tears.

"Because he thinks he can get away with being a dog!" Maya didn't hold back her feelings or her opinion.

"I can't trust him anymore. I was willing to be his everything, but not anymore." I started crying. "Damn it."

"Don't cry, Keysha," Maya said, trying to console me.

"I can't help it," I said as I reached for a tissue. "I thought I was special to him. I felt so connected and so adored when I was with him."

"When I see him again I'm going to go off on him," Maya said.

"Well, you'll have to stand in line behind me."

"Don't shed another tear over that bastard, Keysha.

You can do so much better than him. You're pretty, you're funny and you're a lot of fun to be around. Things are going to get better soon. Just wait and you'll see."

"Thanks for being so encouraging, Maya. I'm just in a real funky place right now," I admitted as I smeared away my tears. "I can't believe I was willing to run away from home just to be with him."

"Don't beat yourself up too much, Keysha. Love will make you do crazy things."

"I trusted him, Maya!" I slammed my fist down on my desk. "How could he betray me like this?"

"Because he's stupid."

"You can say that again," I agreed with her.

"So what are you going to do now?" Maya asked.

"Nothing. I'm not going to call him and I'm certainly not going to take his phone calls for a while. Hopefully he'll get the hint and stop calling altogether. Anyway, thanks for listening to my drama, Maya. I'm going to go take a shower and then go to bed."

"Okay. I'll see you at school. You know they'll be posting the audition results in the cafeteria."

"Girl, I'm not even thinking about the play right now. They're probably going to give the part to Priscilla anyway, so I'm not even going to get my hopes up high, especially with the way my luck has been lately," I said truthfully.

"I'm telling you that you're one hundred percent better than that tramp. If they give the part to Priscilla, I'll have to glue my eyes shut to keep from looking at her because she's so ugly." I laughed out loud at Maya's comment.

"You don't even know if you're in the play yet and you're already talking about having to work with Priscilla."

"Girl, I've been in the school play for the past two years. I'm sure I'll make it again this year," Maya said confidently.

"Well, go on with your bad self," I teased.

"Just don't forget to check the results. You never know, you may have made the cut." Maya was very optimistic.

"Okay, I'll check." I gave in to her confident and positive attitude. I ended my conversation with Maya, turned off my phone and prepared for bed.

When I awoke the next morning, I turned on my cell phone. Wesley had called me several times and left a number of voice mails. I ignored his phone calls and erased his messages. I truly didn't want to hear from him anymore. As far as I was concerned he could go to hell and I wouldn't care. I got out of bed, went into my closet and found the perfect outfit to wear—dark, straight-leg jeans, with a pink cardigan and a matching tank top. I then went into the bathroom, brushed my teeth, washed my face, fussed with my hair and did everything else that I needed to do in order to look as fabulous as possible. I exited the bathroom just as Mike was about to pound on the door and complain about the length of time I was taking.

"It's all yours," I said brightly as I walked past him.

"What's gotten into you?" he asked.

"Nothing, I just feel like being positive today." I was really trying to boost my spirits as much as possible because I was still heartbroken over Wesley. I put on my clothes and headed down to the kitchen. Jordan was standing at the stove frying up some bacon.

"Good morning," he said.

"Good morning," I answered back as I opened the refrigerator door and removed a gallon of milk. I then went to the cupboard and pulled down a box of cereal and prepared my breakfast.

"How are you feeling today?" Jordan asked.

"I'm cool," I answered.

"Just cool? How did the tryouts go?"

"Fine. I read for the part and I'll find out if I made the cut today." I shoveled food into my mouth.

"What's the name of the play? Is it a Shakespeare play?" Jordan asked.

"No. It's some play called *Teenage Love Affair.* I read for the part of the leading lady. My friend Maya read for the part of best friend to the leading lady."

"Well, let me know if you make it," Jordan said as he flipped his food over. A short while later, Barbara and Mike came in and ate breakfast. We all took a little time to chat and catch up on each other's lives. By the time we were finished I didn't have a moment to spare as I gathered up my belongings and headed to school.

I went directly to my locker, hung up my coat and grabbed my materials for class. I closed the locker, making sure my combination lock was securely fastened because kids would break in to your locker if you forgot to firmly snap the lock. As I walked to my class in the crowded hallway, I had to avoid a dispute going on between two girls who were on the verge of getting physical. Once I made it past them I had to deal with the open display of affection that was taking place. Everyone was all boo'd up kissing each other as if they'd never see each other again. My emotions got the best of me and I had to take a detour to the bathroom to get myself together. The last thing I wanted to do was walk down the hallway crying over Wesley. I'd much rather continue doing that in the privacy of my bedroom.

"This is so bogus," I muttered as I glanced at myself in the mirror. "Come on, Keysha girl. Pull it together," I told my reflection. Once I'd calmed down I composed myself and continued on to my first period class.

By lunchtime I was very hungry and rushed to the cafeteria to get in line because if I didn't, it would take forever to get my food.

"Keysha." I heard someone call out my name. I turned and saw Maya rushing toward me.

"Hey, Maya, where's the fire?" I asked, then assumed she wanted to cut in front of me. "Do you want to get in line?"

"You didn't check, did you?" she asked.

"Check what? My phone? Did you send me a text or something?"

"Of course I sent you a text. Why haven't you checked your phone?"

"I don't know. I guess I didn't want to see anything from Wesley, including some sorrowful text message from him."

"Okay, I'm going to help you get over Wesley one way or another." Maya smiled at me as if she was holding on to a secret.

"What?" I asked.

"You made it, Keysha! You made the cut. You're in the play!" Maya couldn't contain her excitement.

"For real?" I'd totally forgotten about the play. I truly didn't take it seriously because I doubted I'd make the cut.

"Yes, I'm for real. Not only did you get in the play, but you got the lead part!" Maya was overjoyed for me. Other students in line congratulated me, but I was truly speechless.

"I actually beat Priscilla?" I was still having a difficult time understanding why I was selected over her.

"I told you, honey. You've got talent that you haven't tapped into yet. Oh, this is so exciting!"

"So what happens next?"

"Practice, girlfriend."

"When does practice begin?" I asked.

"Today after school in the auditorium and you'd better have your behind there."

At the end of the day I phoned Jordan and Barbara to let them know I'd gotten the lead part in the school play and would be coming home later than my usual time. They were both very excited and congratulated me. I also called Grandmother Katie, but got her voice mail. I left a message with the exciting news and asked her to call me back when she could. As I made my way toward the auditorium, I ran into Priscilla, who gave me an ugly look. I ignored her and kept on walking. She'd just have to get over the fact that I got the lead part and she didn't. I opened the doors to the theater. The floor was covered with carpet, which had various autumn-colored patterns. The aisle sloped downward to the wooden stage. All of the house lights and stage lights were brightly lit and as I stood there I began to imagine myself standing on stage giving the performance of a lifetime. In my mind I could hear the roar of a cheering audience.

"Keysha, down here. I saved a seat for you." Maya waved me over to come join her. I walked to where she was and sat.

"We're waiting for a few more people," Maya informed me.

"You'll have to introduce me to everyone because you're the only person I know."

"Don't worry. By the time practice is in full swing you'll know everyone, including the set designers and stage staff."

"I saw that ignorant slut, Priscilla."

"Did she say something to you?" Maya asked.

"No. She just gave me a mean look."

"That's because her ass is jealous. She'll get over it. The theater director picked you because you're more talented."

"I've never considered myself to be talented in this way," I admitted.

"You need to stop staying that. You need to be very confident, especially when the director is offering up constructive criticism. Trust me. This is not a cakewalk by any means. It's going to be hard work and you'll be doing the same scene over and over and over again. It's irritating, but it really helps everyone memorize their lines and develop their characters." Just then, a male student entered the auditorium through a door on the right. I watched as he approached and I had to admit, he was fine.

"Who is that?" I nudged Maya.

"That's Antonio, your leading man." Antonio was incredibly sexy and suave, and walked in with a swagger that said he owned this place. His skin was brown and he had a razor-thin mustache along with well-groomed hair on his chin. His hair was black and wavy and his lips were begging to be kissed. A gold bracelet dangled from his wrist and a gold watch blinged off the lighting near the stage. His lean, muscular body was so sexy.

"He is so hot. I mean straight-up sizzling hot!"

"And he can sing," Maya added.

"For real?" I asked.

"Yeah. He can make a chick drop her panties, but don't get caught up, Keysha. Antonio is all about the booty. I've heard rumors of chicks fighting over him."

"He looks like he's worth fighting for. He could pass for Bow Wow's little brother," I said, admiring his confident strut. As soon as he sat down, Priscilla appeared out of nowhere and sat next to him.

"What's that about?" I asked Maya, who also saw how Priscilla pushed up on Antonio.

"Girl, who knows? She probably wants to become one of his sexual victims." Both Maya and I laughed. "Seriously, though, Antonio is very flirtatious and if you don't watch it, he's the type of brother that can have a girl walking around in circles."

"He can't be that bad," I said as I continued to study him a little more.

"I don't know. I've never been with him and never wanted to, either. Misalo is all the man I need."

"When am I going to meet this Misalo?" I turned my attention back to Maya.

"He asked me the same thing earlier today." Maya laughed. "You'll meet him soon."

Once everyone had arrived, the theater director took roll call and then passed around a sheet of paper, which asked for everyone's contact information. Then she asked that everyone take a little time to stand up and introduce themselves. Once the formalities were taken care of she talked about the play, then gave everyone a copy of the script. We took some time to read it and then started rehearsing the first act. When rehearsal was over I went to gather my belongings.

"Hey."

I turned and saw Antonio approaching me. "Hey," I replied.

"I just wanted to tell you that you're pretty good. You're a natural." Antonio smiled at me while licking his succulent lips.

"Thank you," I said as if his presence had no effect on me whatsoever.

"I'm looking forward to working with you. If you'd like, we could schedule some time to practice our lines since the play is really about our two characters."

"Um, you mean outside of what we're already doing?" I asked for clarification.

"Yeah. You could come over to my place," Antonio suggested. I gave him a condescending look. I wasn't about to fall for that one.

"I don't think so," I said.

"Then I'll come over to your house." He was being persistent.

"You're going to come over to my house?"

"Yeah. I don't have a problem with that unless you do."

"You do realize that you're not setting one foot in my house without my parents being there?" I wanted him to understand that he wasn't going to get any of my goodies.

"Great. I'd love to meet your folks," Antonio said confidently.

"You're a bold one, aren't you?"

"What do you mean?"

"You just act as if you're going to get your way," I explained.

"I'm sort of spoiled like that." He laughed.

"Let me give your visit some thought," I said, smiling at him.

"You do that. I'll see you around," he said and walked away. I went back to my seat, but decided to wait on Maya, who was talking to another student.

"You know, I can't wait for you to mess up," said Priscilla, who sat down in the row behind me.

"Mess up?" I turned and gave her an ugly glare. "What's wrong with you? Why are you tripping, Priscilla?" I asked flat out.

"You suck at this and as soon as you mess up I'm going to be waiting to take your place," she said as she popped her chewing gum.

"Whatever!" I said and ignored her comment.

fourteen

WESLEY

Everything is so messed up and I have no clue
what to do or how to fix it. All I know for sure is that I'm
afraid, angry and on some level vengeful. My dad's car is
a wreck and although I have a strong idea who vandalized his car, I can't prove it. I told my father a guy from
school named Claude might have destroyed the car because I reported him to the principal, but I was only specu-
lating. We made a police report and at the suggestion of
the police, we decided to forward the details to the auto
insurance company and let an adjuster come out to examine the damage.

Then out of the clear blue, someone drove by Lori's
house and opened fire. They found as many as twenty
shell casings from three different guns on the ground in
front of Lori's home. The number of shots fired was a clear
indication that the bandits had one goal in mind, and
that was to kill someone. There were no neighbors on the

street at the time of the shooting and the police were currently doing an investigation.

I tried to call Keysha to explain everything to her, but she refused to answer my call, which was annoying. I wanted to talk to her. I wanted to hear her voice; I wanted her to help me get through the mess I was in, but it was becoming extremely clear that Keysha was putting some distance between us.

While at school today, I thought for sure Claude would catch up with me and start a bunch of bull. However, by lunchtime I hadn't seen him or Lori. While I sat at a lunch table eating, I gave Lori a buzz, but she didn't answer. When the dismissal bell rang I walked by her locker, but she wasn't there. I waited around for her as long as I could, but she never showed up. During my journey home, I strolled past her house and noticed police tape wrapped around the gate. I briefly thought about the last time I'd spoken with her, which was after the police had taken a report of the shooting incident. She was still in a frenzy, but had calmed down a little.

"Everyone here is in shock, Wesley," Lori had begun. "The police said they'll have an extra patrol car drive by the house to make sure the shooters don't come back, but that isn't a comfort to my mother, grandmother, or me," she said, with an uneasy jaggedness in her voice. "My grandmother nearly had a coronary and my mother is still in an emotion tailspin. She's in the other room packing up a suitcase because we're going to stay at a hotel for a few days."

"Why?" I asked

"Because the windows have been shot out for starters,"

Lori scolded me for asking what she considered to be a dumb question.

"Why would someone shoot up your home?" I asked, not understanding the mentality of the individuals who'd done that.

"You know what this is about, Wesley. So stop acting as if you don't. Even my mother understands this is about retaliation. She's doesn't like the fact that I'm involved in your court battle."

"We wouldn't be in court had you not—" I held back my words because I didn't want to say something that I'd regret.

"Had I not what? Made Percy jealous? Is that what you're trying to say? Are you going to place all of the blame on me?"

"I didn't say that, Lori. I just don't think it's right to harass people like this," I said, trying to defuse the brewing spat dancing around our conversation.

"Wesley, when are you going to take off your blinders and realize that gangbangers don't play by the rules? They do whatever they want whenever they want and however they want. Right now they want us dead and they're not going to stop until we're both six feet under."

"That's not going to happen, Lori. I won't let it." I didn't want her to live in fear and uncertainty.

"Yeah, right. You can't stop them, Wesley. None of us can," Lori uttered and then remained silent for a moment before speaking again. "I'll talk to you later. I hear my mother calling me."

"Will you be at school tomorrow?"

"Yeah, I'll be there," Lori said before abruptly disconnecting our call.

* * *

When I walked into the house, my grandmother and father were sitting at the kitchen table. They both looked as if the weight of the world was on their shoulders.

"Hey. What's going on?" I asked as I set my book bag on the countertop.

"Do you want to tell him or do you want me to?" Grandmother Lorraine glanced at my father for a moment.

"You tell him. I'm just incredibly disgusted by this entire situation."

"I spoke with Lori's grandmother today."

"How are they doing? I walked past their house and saw police tape still around the gate."

"They're not coming back for a while," Grandmother Lorraine informed me.

"What do you mean?" I asked.

"Lori and her mother will not be coming back. She didn't tell me where they were going. She just said, 'We're gone.'"

"They just can't pick up and leave at a time like this." I couldn't believe this was happening.

"Yes, they can. Their home is going to be repaired and as soon as it's fixed up it's going to be put on the market for sale."

"That's not the worst of it," my father said. "About an hour after your grandmother got off the phone with Miss Winston, I received a phone call from the state prosecutor. He actually called looking for you, but got me instead. He had Percy's file in front of him and wanted to discuss the details of our criminal case. To make a long story short, Lori's absence puts a nail in the coffin as far as getting a conviction goes. Without Lori's testimony there is no witness who can directly link Percy to the shooting."

"Then let them subpoena her." I figured we'd get Lori involved one way or another.

"You have to know where someone is to serve a subpoena, Wesley. We don't know where Lori is."

"Well, find out from Miss Winston," I said.

"She's not saying a word. She told me that if the police ask her where Lori or her mother is, she's going to simply say she doesn't know," explained Grandmother Lorraine. "Lori and her mother weren't under any court order to remain here in Indianapolis."

"Then let the police track them through bank records or something like that. I've seen them do that a million times on the show *Law & Order*," I suggested.

"Wesley, you're missing the point, son. The police aren't going to do that because Lori and her mom haven't committed a crime. They're not under investigation. If the subpoena had been served before they left, it would be different. But it wasn't."

"So what are you saying? Percy is going get away with this? He gets to shoot me and nothing happens to him!" I was really ticked off.

Dad took a deep breath and then exhaled. "The prosecutor says that we have a very weak case and the chances of a conviction are very slim. I'm just as upset and ticked off about this as you are. But our hands are tied."

"What if Lori comes back? What if I find her and get her to testify?"

"I didn't ask that question, but I suppose it would only help to build a stronger case. However, if her parents don't want her to get involved, Wesley, there isn't much we can do about it."

I paused in thought. "So what's to stop Percy from getting out of jail and shooting me again? This is crazy! I might as well get a gun and blow his damn head off myself!" I howled out like a roaring lion.

"Percy isn't getting out of jail." My dad met my roar with one of his own before he went on to give more details.

"What are you talking about?" I asked.

"When the police picked Percy up for questioning they found drugs on him, which was a violation of his parole."

"Wait a minute. Percy was on parole? What for?"

"The prosecutor wouldn't tell me. He was being generous when he shared that information. He said that Percy is not likely to be getting out anytime soon."

"So what happens now?" I asked, feeling as if I'd just gotten screwed over by our broken judicial system.

"Our house will be ready next week. We'll be going home. Your grandmother is also going to come and stay with us for a while. Just until some of the tension here settles down."

"Good, because I hate this town. I can't wait to get out of this crazy madhouse of a city!" I spoke from my heart before heading to my room to ponder my predicament of defeat and disgrace.

"Wesley, we haven't lost. We'll file a civil lawsuit." Dad was unwilling to concede to defeat.

"If you say so, Dad." As I steadied my balance to

descend the staircase, my shoulder began to ache. I made a mental note to talk to my dad about setting up therapy sessions once we returned home.

fifteen

KEYSHA

sometimes I gaze into my own eyes and wonder if I have the courage to get through a particular set of circumstances. This morning I awoke with an achy pain in my heart. My distress started off very subtle, but as I arose from my bed the feeling began to grow. When I took a moment to truly acknowledge the throbbing sensation, I diagnosed my condition as a broken heart. Over the past few days I'd been so angry with Wesley that I hadn't really given myself a chance to grieve the loss of my relationship with him. However, on this day, my heart decided it was time for me to shed some tears over a guy who meant the world to me. I went into the bathroom, grabbed a face towel and took my usual position on the rim of the bathtub. I slumped my head between my legs and began to sob. I tried to cry quietly, but once my emotions gained control over me, silent mourning wasn't possible. There was a light knock on the bathroom door.

"Hey, are you okay in there?" Mike's ears were obviously sensitive to my crying.

"I'm fine," I said, trying to assure him.

"You sound like a wounded wolf. Are you sure?"

"Mike, I'm okay, just a little emotional this morning. I'm cramping up," I lied so he'd leave me alone.

"Oh. My bad." I'd embarrassed him—I could tell by the way his footsteps hurriedly moved away from the door. Once I'd had a good cry about Wesley, I wrangled up my dribbling emotions and put them in check as best as I could. Then I prepared for what was surely going to be a very long school day.

At the end of the day I walked to Maya's locker. Her boyfriend Misalo was already there kissing her lustfully. Their tongues were dancing inside of each other's mouths in perfect rhythm. A little too flawless if you ask me, because they hadn't noticed me gawking at them.

"Ahem..." I cleared my throat so they'd cease their public display of affection.

"Girl!" Maya turned to see who was interrupting her make-out session. "You shouldn't walk up on me like that. I was about to beat you down for interfering with my blissful moment."

"Sorry about that," I answered, slightly jealous of the fact that Maya had a boyfriend and I didn't.

"Keysha, this is my boo, Misalo," Maya said, finally introducing us. Misalo was a rather interesting-looking guy. He had silky-smooth chocolate-brown skin, downy lips and curly ringlets of black hair, which looked handsomely beautiful on him.

"Hi. It's nice to finally meet you." He smiled then extended his hand. I reached out to shake it.

"It's nice to meet you, as well," I said, suddenly thinking about what Maya had told me about wanting to have sex with him. If I were his girlfriend I must admit the thought would have certainly crossed my mind. Especially since he had a spectacular grade of hair. Misalo said goodbye and Maya watched him as he walked away.

"He is so hot and you guys make the perfect couple," I said, giving Maya my honest opinion of their union.

"I know, and I constantly have to fight the chickenheads who want a piece of him," Maya complained. "Even the grown women look at him as if they'd eat him up if he wasn't so young. But I told him if I ever catch him with another girl, I'm going to do what Rihanna should've done to Chris Brown and start cutting off body parts," Maya said as she closed her locker, making sure it was securely shut.

"Are you ready for practice?" I asked as we moved down the corridor toward the auditorium.

"I guess. I was late trying to memorize my lines," Maya said.

"So was I. But I fell asleep from exhaustion. I had so much homework to do," I whined.

"Well, you'd better find some energy and quick because you have a lot of lines to learn and the director expects you to know them by heart." Maya explained the intensity of the work that was on the road ahead.

"But, Maya, my teachers are loading me up with a ton of bull. I have papers, tests and lab projects. I'm starting to go crazy with the workload."

"You're not the only one trying to juggle a mountain of work." Maya laughed a little. "Relax, Keysha. You're going to get through this," Maya said as we entered the auditorium.

We walked toward the stage and placed our book bags in an empty seat. The director made sure that everyone had a dialogue sheet and then asked the characters from the opening scene to go onto the stage. Antonio and I went on stage. I sat in a chair on one side of the stage and he sat in a chair at the opposite end. The director instructed the light crew how to light the stage with one spotlight illuminating each of us. Then I was asked to read my lines. When I was finished the director gave me some strong criticism about my delivery and asked me to do it again, and again and again until I was sick and tired of hearing my own voice. Once the director was done with me, he moved on to Antonio. Once we were done, I went back to my seat to watch Maya perform.

"So when are we going to hook up for a practice session?" Antonio asked as he sat down next to me. I glanced at him and the only thing I could think about was kissing him. "How does Saturday at noon sound to you?" he asked.

Sometimes, when I'm nervous, I talk too fast and my tongue flops around in my mouth. My words sounded awful, like a cartoon character's once an anvil had been dropped on his head. "That's sounds fine," I said nervously. I took a breath and repeated myself. "That sounds like a great idea," I answered. "Where would you like to meet?"

"Why don't we meet here at the school? I'm sure the auditorium will be open," Antonio suggested.

"Okay," I said, not putting up much of a fight. Antonio and I watched every performance. There were several times when his leg rested against my own. I didn't know if he was touching me purposely or if he honestly didn't realize it. Either way, I didn't say anything. I just quietly enjoyed the feel of his strong leg resting against me. I closed my eyes and fantasized about the two of us sitting alone in the darkened auditorium kissing and touching each other. I imagined myself surrendering to his strong embrace while enjoying the scent of some expensive cologne he was wearing. I inhaled deeply a few times before I was jolted out of my daydream by a sharp kick to the back of my seat. I immediately turned around.

"Oh, I'm sorry about that," Priscilla said, offering up a fake apology. "My leg just jerks like that sometimes."

"Kick my seat again and you're getting a beat down," I threatened.

"Shh!" The director turned in his seat and gave me an evil look.

"It wasn't me," I quickly said, but he didn't seem to care who it was; he just wanted silence while he worked with Maya and several other performers. I turned my attention back to Priscilla, who had a smug smile on her face that I wanted to slap off.

"You shouldn't be sitting there anyway," she whispered, still wanting to aggravate me.

"Last time I checked it was a free country, and a person could sit down anywhere they pleased," I asserted in a hushed whisper.

"I know what you're trying to do and—"

"Priscilla! Will you just chill out?" Antonio finally turned around in his seat and said something.

"No, I won't chill out," Priscilla snapped at him.

"Hey! Be *quiet* while they're on stage!" the director snapped at us.

"I need to get some air," Antonio said, rising to his feet. He walked up the aisle and exited the theater.

"Priscilla, you're onstage next," said the director.

"Now watch and learn from a real actress at work. I'll nail my lines on the first take," Priscilla boldy affirmed as she made her way to the stage.

When I arrived home it was almost eight o'clock in the evening. I walked into the house and kicked my shoes off at the door. I lugged my book bag up the stairs and into the family room, where Jordan was sitting on the sofa snuggled up with Barbara watching a movie they'd rented. Jordan hit the pause button.

"How did it go?" he asked.

"Yeah, what was it like?" asked Barbara.

"Long," I whined. "I've really got to learn my part. I've got to learn how to step into character and project my voice. I had to keep reading the same lines over and over and over again until I got it right."

"It sounds like this is going to be a real challenge for you," Barbara said as she rose to her feet. She walked past me and into the kitchen.

"Challenge is an understatement," I said.

"I left your dinner on the stove. You can heat it up once

you get settled in." Barbara opened up the refrigerator and removed a cold soda.

"I'll come back down and reheat it. Right now I need to get upstairs and start on my homework." I was about to drag my book bag up to my room.

"Why don't you use my office, Keysha? It's easy to fall asleep when you're doing homework while sitting on your bed."

"Fine," I griped as I lugged my belongings back down the stairs and into Jordan's office.

After eating dinner and drinking two energy drinks, I'd gotten a good jolt of adrenaline and I began doing my homework. However, about a few hours later, I crashed so badly I fell asleep sitting upright in Jordan's desk chair. Eventually, Jordan came into the room and woke me up.

"Keysha," he said, shaking my shoulder.

"What?" I answered groggily.

"Go get into your bed. It's midnight," he said.

"Mid-what?" My mind was still in a fog.

"Go to bed. Come on." Jordan helped me stand on my feet and then guided me out of his office and out of the basement. I lazily walked up the stairs and into my bedroom. As soon as my head landed on my pillow, I drifted off into a deep sleep.

sixteen

WESLEY

saturday morning arrived and no one was more eager to hit the highway and head back home than me. I woke up early to allow myself enough time to pack up what belongings I could. Having the use of only one arm presented me with more challenges than I initially thought it would. However, I'd arisen confident and enthusiastic about returning to my old neighborhood, visiting with Keysha and clearing the air between us. Earlier during the week, my father visited with my counselor, who provided him with a copy of my transcript and other necessary paperwork for me to take back to Thornwood High. His car had been returned from the repair shop. They'd replaced the shattered glass, but hadn't repainted the car yet. Dad said he knew of a place back home that would take care of repainting his car.

Grandmother Lorraine wasn't as frantic as I was about returning to Illinois. In fact she grumbled continually about having to leave home.

"I feel as if I'm being run out of my house." She raised her voice in opposition to the decision my father had made for her. In spite of my dad's indifference to her complaints, Grandmother Lorraine didn't put up too much of a fight and packed for what I believed was going to be an extended stay.

Dad spoke with Mr. Stein, a short, potbellied man who was the head of the neighborhood watch club. Mr. Stein was fond of walking his dog at odd hours of the night. This proved to be beneficial to Grandmother Lorraine; my dad had gotten him to agree to keep an eye on the house and to alert us, as well as the authorities, if he saw anything suspicious. Dad provided Mr. Stein with a few contact numbers and thanked him for his neighborly kindness.

After I'd packed up several small suitcases and two oversize duffel bags, I checked around once again to make sure I wasn't leaving anything of value or importance behind. I then made several trips back and forth from the basement to the car, where I stuffed everything in the trunk. We were finally on our way around 1:00 p.m. We made one stop at a local gas station, where both Dad and Grandmother Lorraine filled up their gas tanks. I ran inside and grabbed a giant bag of gummy worms, potato chips and two sodas for Dad and me to snack on during the three-hour journey back home.

As we drove away from the noise and congestion of the city, the landscape of tall buildings and multilane highways gave way to farmland and just two lanes to zoom along on.

"I can't wait to see the house." Dad struck up a conversation to break the silence.

"Same here," I said, fumbling with the radio in search of some type of decent music to listen to.

"The contractor said everything is working and we wouldn't be able to tell there was ever a fire in the house."

"I'm just looking forward to sleeping in my own bed." I finally came across a rock station.

"Wait! Leave it there. I love that song," he said as he began to sing along with an old Phil Collins song called "In the Air Tonight."

"I was dating a girl named Kris when this song was out. We used to love slow dancing to this song. She was tall and had strawberry-blond hair. Kris had freckles, a pretty smile and was incredibly intelligent. Her hips were like two sacred stones, identifying the entrance to all of her secrets," my dad said, shaking his head as if clearly seeing what happened in the past.

I frowned at my father's poetic words. "TMI, Dad."

"What does TMI mean?" he asked, completely perplexed.

"Too much information. I don't need to know about the woman's hips," I said, although I fully understood his fascination with that particular part of the female anatomy. Dad laughed.

"Anyway, Kris loved to dance and back then your old man was a dancing *machine*." He laughed as he became lost in nostalgia.

I humored him and asked, "Whatever happened to her?"

"She moved away. And I lost contact with her. I heard through the grapevine that she'd become some kind of scientist."

"Liked the brainy type, eh?" I teased him.

"A smart woman is very sexy."

"You should get a Facebook account and see if you can find her," I suggested as Phil Collins belted out "Oh, Lord" in his husky voice.

"What's Facebook?" he asked. I laughed because I couldn't believe he hadn't heard of the social networking Web site.

"Come on, Dad, you've got to keep up, man. You have to live in the twenty-first century. The eighties are over and gone."

"There is no need to be cynical, Wesley. Is it like MySpace?" he asked.

"Yeah, it's like MySpace and sort of like Twitter," I explained. "Whenever we get a new computer I'll show you how it's done."

"Once we get settled in, we'll go on a shopping spree to replace the furniture that was lost in the fire. I'm positive there will be enough money in the budget for a new computer."

"Cool. I want a laptop." I grinned as I put in my request. Dad and I settled into a comfortable silence.

"Oh, did I tell you that I'll be going back to work soon?"

"No. Are you well enough to go back?" I asked, glancing over at his hands, which were still pink from his burns.

"Yeah, I'll be able to go back at the end of the month. I can't wait to get back to work because sitting around all day was driving me crazy," he admitted.

"I'm sure all of your coworkers will throw you a nice welcome-back celebration," I said.

"That would be nice, but it's really not necessary."

Dad clicked his turn signal and switched lanes. We talked the remainder of the way home. Occasionally we were interrupted by Grandmother Lorraine, who needed to stop at every oasis along the way for a bathroom break. It was an inconvenience, but we had to be accommodating to her needs.

We finally pulled into the driveway of our home. The house looked nothing like it did the last time I saw it. The black burn marks were gone, the windows had been replaced and the place genuinely looked welcoming. As soon as Dad put the car in Park, I got out of the car, removed my door keys from my pants pocket and stepped inside. The house smelled like fresh paint and new carpet. The scents of charred furnishings and moldy-smelling water were long gone. I walked down the stairs and into the basement, which had been completely overhauled. There was new drywall, a new ceiling and a new furnace, washer, dryer and hot water tank. I hustled back up the stairs and back out to the driveway. Dad was wheeling Grandmother Lorraine's suitcase toward the front door.

"I'll get the rest of the stuff out of the trunk," I said, eager to unload everything and get settled in.

An hour later, I was standing before my dresser drawer, putting away the last of my clothes. Once my task was complete, I rested on my bed and relaxed. My shoulder ached like hell. I gave myself another reminder to set up a new therapy schedule.

I then decided it was time to phone Keysha and surprise her with my return. I was optimistic about getting a chance to come over and visit with her for a while. If an afternoon visit wasn't possible, I hoped she'd at least be more receptive to hearing my apology. I pulled out my cell phone, held it in my hand and glared at it mindlessly for a moment. I was suddenly afraid to call her because I feared she'd either ignore my call or answer it and scream at me like a lunatic. Finally, I gathered up the courage to give her a jingle.

"Hello," Keysha answered, laughing. It was so nice to hear her in good spirits.

"Hey, how is it going?" I asked nervously, not sure of how she'd react.

"Who is this?" she asked, still chuckling. I could hear noise in the background. It sounded as if there was some type of celebration taking place.

"Did I catch you at a bad time?"

"Wesley?"

"Yes," I answered. There was a long moment of silence.

"What are you up to?" she finally asked.

"Nothing," I answered. The fact that she didn't hang up on me was in my opinion a positive sign. "Guess what?"

"Wesley, I really don't have time for games." I guess Keysha didn't want to play along with me.

"Okay," I said, feeling as if I suddenly meant nothing to her.

"If you have something to say, go ahead. If not, I've got to get back to Antonio."

"Antonio!" I scowled, feeling jealousy rise within me like a balloon being filled with air. "Who is Antonio?"

"Why does it matter to you, Wesley?"

"Because…it does. Why is he over there?" I wanted to know.

"I invited him over. You got a problem with that?" Keysha said.

"As a matter of fact, I do," I replied.

"Whatever, Wesley. I've got to go." Keysha was about to hang up on me.

"Wait." I stopped her.

"What?" she asked impatiently.

"When can I see you? I'm back at home now."

"Really? When did you get back?"

"This afternoon. I was hoping I could see you so I can clear the air between us," I said, hoping for an opportunity to speak to her face-to-face.

"I'm very busy these days, Wesley."

"Come on, Keysha. You at least have to give me a chance to say I'm sorry." Keysha's silence meant she was considering it.

"Please. I would apologize over the phone, but I'd like to do it in person. Are you busy on Sunday?"

"Yes. Barbara, Jordan, Mike and I are driving up to Gurnee Mills to do some shopping."

"I have to wait until Monday to see you?" I whined.

"Looks that way," Keysha answered with indifference.

"Well, can I see you first thing Monday? I could meet you at your locker."

"Fine," Keysha answered. "I've got to go. It's rude of me to be on the phone when I have a guest visiting. I'll talk to you later."

"Keysha. I love— Hello?" Keysha disconnected the call

before I had a chance to tell her how I truly felt. I punched my mattress a few times with my left fist. I was frustrated and resentful of the fact she didn't want to see me. Even more frustrating was the reality of having to compete for her affections with some new guy.

seventeen

KEYSHA

when I hung up the phone I turned my attention back to Antonio, Maya and Misalo, who were over visiting. We'd moved the leather furniture around and created an area that we pretended was a stage. Maya and Misalo would sit in two fold-up chairs that I brought up from the basement while Antonio and I stood before them and practiced our lines. I would be lying to myself if I said I wasn't attracted to Antonio. He had a good sense of humor and was easy to get along with. He was charming, charismatic and had alluring eyes that seemed to say more than his mouth was willing to admit.

Earlier, when Antonio arrived, I asked Barbara to answer the door because I didn't want to show too much zeal over his visit. Barbara thought I was being silly until I told her I wanted her to take a look at him and let me know what her first impression of him was. When Antonio arrived Barbara opened the door.

"Hello. You must be Keysha's sister, right?" Antonio immediately won Barbara over by bathing her with compliments.

"No. I'm not her sister. I'm her mother." Barbara chuckled as she invited him inside.

"No way!" Antonio shouted out, seemingly surprised.

"Yeah way!" Barbara matched the loudness of his voice with her own.

"You do not look like you have a daughter as old as Keysha."

"I'm not trying to look old, either."

"Trust me, you don't. If I were a little older I'd certainly ask you for a date." Antonio flirted with Barbara, who suddenly began snickering like a featherbrained schoolgirl.

"Oh, really? Too bad you're catching me on a bad day. You should see me when I'm all fixed up." I stuck my finger down my throat and pretended to puke. I couldn't believe Barbara was actually flirting back with him. I made a mental note to remind Jordan that he needed to pay more attention to her.

"Earth to Keysha, are you there?" Maya teased me and snapped me out of my flashback.

"I'm sorry, I'm just spacing out."

"Well, you need to stay here on Planet Popular People with Antonio, Misalo and me." Everyone laughed at Maya's comment.

"Okay, where were we?" Antonio still had the script in his hand.

"Um, we left off right here…where the lovers are about to kiss each other," I said. Now, up until this point,

Antonio and I had never really kissed. The way we'd practiced it was as follows—a spotlight would come up on us as we stood center stage. Then we'd say our lines and lean in toward each other, stopping just short of a kiss before the stage lights would go down and the stage crew would come out and hurriedly change the set. I was, without question, all set to do it the way we practiced until Misalo made a suggestion.

"You guys should really kiss each other. That would be so hot and I'm sure the audience would feel the passion the characters have for each other."

"For a guy who doesn't speak very much, it's kind of awkward to hear you say something so daring," I teasingly mocked him.

"I think he's got a point there," Maya chimed in.

"What?" I said.

"I'm serious. It would be incredibly hot if you guys actually kissed. I mean it doesn't have to be anything serious. Just let your lips touch," Maya said.

"Yeah, go ahead and do that." Misalo had a grin on his face like a cat who'd just saw a birdcage door snap open.

"I'm willing to give it a try if you are," Antonio said.

"I can't. My mom is in the other room. Are you guys crazy?" I said, scowling at them.

"Oh, give it a try, Keysha. We'll keep an eye out. Besides, the kiss is only going to be for a split second. But you've got to make it look real or it won't work." Maya rose to her feet, grabbed her purse and took out some breath mints.

"Here. This way no one gets offended by bad breath," Maya said as Antonio started laughing.

"If I kiss Keysha for real, she might fall in love with me," he said.

"Don't count on it," I said in an attempt to crush his overinflated ego. However, I will admit the thought of his pillow-soft lips pressing against my own was rather appealing. I took the breath mint Maya had given me and sucked on it before splitting it into tiny pieces with my teeth while I chewed away the remaining particles. Antonio stood opposite me and did the same.

"Are you ready?" I asked.

"You're positive you want to do this?" Antonio gave me one final warning.

"You're not getting cold feet, are you?" I challenged him. He smirked and then glanced down at his lines. When Maya gave us our cue, Antonio and I stepped into character and read our lines. Instantaneously, I transformed myself into the main character. I became the brokenhearted girl who was in anguish because her parents forbade her to see her boyfriend because he was of a different race. The character's parents had finalized plans to send her to live with a relative on the other side of the country.

"I won't listen to them and I'm certainly not going to leave you, my love." I frowned, fully submerged in the feelings of my character.

"I hate people like your parents! They are evil and wicked and don't understand that true love is color-blind." Antonio also became his character.

"No, they don't." I turned my back to Antonio and paused. "That is why I've decided to escape from my oppressive home to be with you."

"We can't be with each other. You know as much as I do that I could never provide for you the way they can." Antonio approached me from behind. He reached out and touched my shoulder. I turned to face him.

"I don't care about materialistic things. All I want is you. Don't you know that?" Antonio looked down at me and I looked up at him. His lips were smooth and inviting.

"And I want you as well, my love." Our lips traveled slowly toward each other. I could feel the warmth of his breath heating my skin and it felt heavenly. Exotic butterflies began dancing around in my tummy as I surrendered to him. I wanted to be with Antonio the moment I saw him. In the privacy of my own mind I'd kissed him a thousand times. When his soft lips met mine, they tasted sweet, like ripe mangoes full of sweet juice. I inhaled the delicious scent of Antonio's cologne as he embraced me tightly. His kiss became more passionate and our tongues did a circular waltz, which was so wonderful, I melted like ice cream sitting on a tabletop in the warm summer sun.

That night, I lay in bed replaying the kiss Antonio and I had over and over again in my mind. I felt as if I had a videotape and kept rewinding it so that I could remember every hot and steamy detail. Antonio was a good kisser. No, he was better than a good kisser; he was a magnificent kisser.

Still, I didn't allow things to get too far out of hand. After all, Barbara was in the other room and I would've been completely horrified if she had walked in at the exact moment Antonio and I were kissing. I was also thankful

Jordan wasn't home. He'd gone into the office to work on some report and Mike had gone to see a movie with his girlfriend, Sabrina.

On Sunday, while I was out shopping with Barbara, Jordan and Mike, I received several text messages from Antonio. He told me how much he enjoyed his visit, and how he looked forward to more and, of course, the mesmerizing kiss we shared. I was glad he was thinking about me and I honestly was looking forward to seeing him again at rehearsal. I couldn't wait to kiss him again in front of Priscilla, so that she could turn green with envy.

When Monday morning arrived, I was still buzzing from the kiss and began to think about what it would be like to be Antonio's girlfriend. For starters, I knew right away I'd have to fend off all the sluts, tramps and hoochie mamas who'd try to steal him away from me. I began to wonder if I could handle throngs of girls crowding around him as if he were some celebrity.

I walked to school with Mike, who was complaining about how much Sabrina was bossing him around and how annoying it was. I listened and offered him a little advice, which he considered to be helpful. As we walked across the school parking lot, Mike saw a friend and said he'd catch me later.

When I entered the building and walked down the corridor past the library, I saw Wesley standing near my locker. His arm was in a sling, but he had a bushel of flowers in the other. My heart began racing; for starters I'd forgotten that I'd agreed to meet with him, and two, I suddenly felt a little sorry for him.

"These are for you," he said, handing me the flowers. They were multicolored carnations, the kind that are sold at the nearby grocery store.

"Thank you. They're pretty," I said, taking them and smelling them. "How does your arm feel?" I asked.

He raised his arm up and then put it back down. "It's okay. It stiffens up a lot and it still hurts when I take it out of the sling. But overall, I can tell that it's healing up. I only have to wear the sling for a few more weeks. I've set up some therapy appointments, which will help. So, how have you been?"

I sighed and shifted my weight from one foot to the other. "Pretty good, considering all that I've gone through." I coyly reminded him of the lengths I'd gone through to get to him.

"What you've gone through? You have no idea of the hell I've had to endure."

"Well, you didn't go through it alone. You had that Lori chick there to help you."

"Keysha, I've missed you. Lori is just a friend."

"You must think I'm a total fool, Wesley." I scowled at him for insulting my intelligence.

"No, I don't. I'm telling you the truth. She was just a girl in the neighborhood."

"And a girl you took a bullet for. Let's not forget that."

"I would've done the same for you, Keysha, and you know that."

"Whatever, Wesley. If you've got something to say, just say it."

"What's that supposed to mean?" I could hear him getting angry.

"It's okay that you have another girlfriend, Wesley. I'm over it now. I've thought about it, cried about it and I'm over it."

"Keysha, I don't even know where Lori is. You don't understand the full story."

"I understand enough," I countered.

"Wait a minute. We're starting off all wrong here. I want you to know that I love you, Keysha."

"Wesley, don't say things that you don't mean."

"I'm serious. I've missed you so much. Haven't you been getting my phone calls?"

I thought about it for a moment and I had to admit Wesley did call me an awful lot.

"Yeah, I got your phone calls," I confessed as I opened my locker and grabbed what I needed and then closed it.

"Am I still your boyfriend?" Wesley asked. I stared into his pretty eyes for a second, searching for honesty and sincerity.

"Can I have another chance?" he asked. I was about to say maybe when I heard some girl call out his name.

"Wesley, is that you?" I turned in the direction of the voice and was flabbergasted when I saw Lori. She came up to him, hugged him tightly and then gave him a quick peck on the lips.

"I'm so sorry. I've missed you so much," Lori continued. Wesley looked like a deer caught in headlights.

"You're such a liar and a jackass, Wesley!" I said as I tossed his crappy cheap flowers at him.

eighteen

WESLEY

"**ouch!**" Lori cried out when the flowers Keysha had tossed at me hit her as well. "Who tossed these?" Lori asked, playing dumb, as if she didn't see me talking to Keysha before she walked up to me.

"Didn't you see me talking to Keysha when you walked up?" I growled at Lori.

"No! The only person I saw was you." Lori tried to convince me that she was totally focused on me. "I thought you'd be happy to see me," Lori said, pouting because she wasn't getting the reaction she'd hoped for.

"Oh, why is my life so damn complicated?" I uttered and then repositioned my body to rest my back against the lockers. Lori looked down the crowded hallway for Keysha, but she was long gone.

"So, were you trying to make up with her?" Lori asked, but seeing the flowers should've given her the answer to that question.

"What do you think?" I snarled, displeased with the fact she'd interrupted what was supposed to be the perfect reunion of two lovers.

"The next time she throws something at me she'd better be prepared for a fight. In fact, when I see her again I'm just going to walk up to her and knock her out." Lori's eyes were ablaze with anger and revenge.

"Damn!" I barked as I began to think about how I was going to make this up to Keysha.

"Well, Wesley?" Lori was still waiting for me to acknowledge her presence in a more satisfactory way. I glared at her for a moment, utterly puzzled.

"I'm doing just fine. Thanks for asking," Lori said, putting words in my mouth. I suppose she wanted me to ask how she was doing.

"What are you doing here, Lori?" I finally snapped out of my daze and accepted the fact that she hadn't disappeared off the face of the earth as her grandmother, Miss Winston, had led my dad and I to believe.

"Yes, Wesley, I'm happy to see you as well. In fact I've been thinking about you constantly," Lori answered, still asserting the notion that I was missing the romantic importance of our seeing each other again.

"You know what? You're too much for me. I'll catch you later." I'd finally had enough of her and walked away. Lori wasn't about to let me turn my back on her so she followed me.

"Where are you going?" she asked as she moved quicker to keep pace with my stride.

"To the registration office. Today is my first day back and I need to get registered."

"Is your house all fixed now?" Lori continued to ask questions. She was like a fly at a picnic who didn't realize she'd worn out her welcome.

I stopped walking. "Why do you even care, Lori? You and your family ran out! Percy isn't going to jail for shooting me because you, my star witness, skipped town. As far as I'm concerned, you and I don't have a damn thing to discuss, so why don't you just get lost?"

She pointed her index finger at me and poked me on the chest. "You listen here, jerk-off! They shot up my grandmother's house. My mother, grandmother and I were in the house watching television when all of a sudden glass began shattering. Neither my mother or grandmother knew what was happening and they were about to pull back the curtain to see who'd thrown an object at our window. I shouted at them to get on the floor before they got shot! My grandmother didn't believe someone was shooting and thought it was just boys playing with fireworks. I had to rush over and push her to the floor before a bullet nailed her between the eyes. So spare me all of your self-righteous bull because you're not the only victim here!"

"Lori, you're a tragedy and the more I hang around with you the more my life continues to spiral out of control. You're like some bad rash or virus that keeps spreading."

"Screw you, Wesley!" she yelled out. Other students who were passing by stopped to watch the drama unfold.

"Whatever! Just leave me alone," I shouted and tried to put some more distance between us.

* * *

Once I got registered, my counselor, Mr. Saunders, assigned me a locker and wrote down my classes for me. He used a special intercom system and called directly into my first period biology class to inform the teacher that I'd been assigned to her class. Mr. Saunders then gave me a hallway pass before sending me on my way. I picked up my backpack and tossed it over my good shoulder.

"Do you need any help getting to class?" asked Mr. Saunders, clearly sympathetic to my injured shoulder.

"No. I've got it," I assured him before continuing on.

As I walked through the hallway I noticed security guards patrolling the halls in greater numbers. I had to show each of them my pass as I traveled from one hallway to the next. When I entered biology class the teacher greeted me and told me to take a seat in the back row. As I walked toward my seat, I noticed that I'd been assigned to a seat next to Lori.

"Oh, you've got to be kidding me," I muttered. Lori glanced at me. Her eyes were red and swollen and it was unmistakably clear she'd been crying. I quickly looked around to see if there was another seat, but there wasn't. The classroom was full. I exhaled, took my seat and tried not to say a word.

"Lori, until I'm able to get a book for Wesley would you mind sharing with him?" asked the biology teacher, Ms. Vogt. I thought for sure Lori was going to protest, but she didn't. As quietly as she could, she scooted her chair next to mine, and pointed to the section we were reading.

I didn't say anything to Lori during the entire class.

When the dismissal bell rang I gathered up my belongings and headed to my next class. I felt as if I was being punished for something I didn't know about; I'd also been assigned a seat directly in front of Lori for English class. I tried to ignore her, but it was impossible. She kept sniffling, wiping her nose and drying her eyes.

The English teacher, Mr. Abraham, asked everyone to pull out their journals and write what was written on the blackboard. I pulled out a spiral notebook from my backpack along with a pen, and as carefully as I could began the process of trying to write with my left hand. It was a frustrating struggle to say the least. By the time the dismissal bell rang, I hadn't been able to copy down much. While everyone began to leave, I tried to memorize what was written on the blackboard.

"Here. I'm not the evil bitch you think I am. I copied it all for you," Lori said as she handed me two sheets of paper containing the information I needed. At that particular moment, my feelings went from somewhere between vexed and hateful to grateful and sympathetic.

"What's your next class?" Lori asked. I removed a crumpled piece of paper from my pocket and took a look. I hesitated before giving her an answer.

"World history with Mr. Thomas." I waggled in my stance as I jerked my duffel bag onto my shoulder.

"It's just like I said before—fate is bringing us together."

"Excuse me?" I couldn't hear what she was mumbling about because I wasn't paying close attention.

"Magnets, Wesley. We are like magnets," Lori concluded with confidence.

"What are you talking about?" I asked, trying to make sense of her babbling.

"I have world history with Mr. Thomas as well."

"You're kidding me, right?" I hoped she was lying.

"No, I'm not," Lori stammered before sharing how she believed destiny was uniting us. "All magnets have north-seeking and south-seeking poles. When magnets are placed near each other, opposite poles attract and like poles repel each other. When the north polarities of magnets are facing each other they repel away. But when a north and south polarity meet there is an instant attraction and a strong bond."

"So, what are you saying? We're really attached to each other, but we've just gotten on each other's bad side?" I tried to bring meaning and understanding to her scientific assessment of our complicated relationship.

"Yes. I'm trying to say that is what I believe," Lori humbly answered. I searched her eyes and knew she was being as truthful as she knew how.

"So what now?" I wanted to be brazen and disrespectful toward her. After all she'd put me through she certainly had it coming. Yet, I felt compelled to at least hear her out and get her side of the story.

"If you'd just give me fifteen minutes of your time to explain myself it would mean the world to me," she said.

"I can do that."

"Meet me after school at Mr. Submarine. We can talk there," she suggested. I accepted her invitation.

When school let out, I gathered up my belongings and headed across the campus toward Mr. Submarine. Just as she'd promised, Lori was already there and had taken the liberty of ordering us some food.

"I saw you walking over here through the window so I ordered you something to eat. I figured that you might be hungry," Lori said as I sat down and joined her. "I hope you like turkey."

"Yeah, I like it," I admitted as I uncovered the sandwich before me. Needless to say I felt as if I was starving. My dad and grandmother hadn't gotten a chance to stock up on groceries.

"So, after the police did their investigation and everything, my mother flipped totally out. She didn't want to have anything to do with you or the court case. She became paranoid and thought for sure the gangbangers would come back and break in to the house during the middle of the night and do all kinds of god-awful things. Her panicky attitude drove me crazy."

"I can understand how that could make her feel rather paranoid," I said, biting into my sandwich.

"You don't understand. My mother can be a real basket case. She called up my father and pleaded with him to let us come stay with him. My father didn't want to deal with my mom and her drama, but she wore him down. He finally consented to my mother, grandmother and me staying with him for a while. My mother is using it as an opportunity to get back into my father's good graces, but..." Lori lowered her head, shut her eyes and remained silent. I could tell she was struggling with more than she was willing to share with me. "Anyway, I'm here now. I'm away from Percy and all of the drama I'd gotten tangled up in with him. No one really knows me here and I guess in some ways that's a good thing, right?" Lori glanced at me for confirmation.

"I don't know. I guess so," I replied, unaware of the answer she was seeking.

"How is that shoulder of yours doing?" Lori asked, changing the subject.

"I can't wait to get out of this damn sling. My shoulder is really stiff and I find myself constantly rubbing it."

"Really? You should let me rub it for you. I give good massages." Lori rose to her feet and positioned herself behind me. She placed her hands on my shoulders and began rubbing them. I'd be lying if I said her touch didn't feel good. She coaxed away a lot of the embedded tension deep within my muscles. It didn't take long for my mind to slip into a mildly euphoric state. With my eyes closed and my chin craned toward my chest, I enjoyed the moment of tenderness.

"Can you forgive me, Wesley?" Lori leaned down and whispered in my ear. "Please."

"I'm trying to," I said.

"I want you to know that I'm willing to do whatever it takes to make all of this up to you. And Wesley...I do mean *whatever it takes*." Lori nibbled on my earlobe and placed sweet kisses on my neck, which sent goose bumps of pleasure racing all over my body.

nineteen

KEYSHA

when the dismissal bell rang, I was relieved. I exited my classroom and merged into the flow of hallway traffic and listened to multiple conversations about hanging out at Mr. Submarine, the nearby pizza parlor and the highway oasis perched high above Interstate 80. While everyone was planning an afternoon of freedom from the oppression of teachers and administrators I had to hustle down to the auditorium for rehearsals. I'd been sending text messages to Maya throughout the day, giving her the blow-by-blow of what transpired between Wesley and me. Like me, she couldn't believe Lori was a student here at Thornwood. When I entered the auditorium, Maya was sitting in one of the house seats, far away from the stage. When I spotted her, she waved me over.

"When I got your text message I was like, '*No freaking way!*'" Maya couldn't wait to gossip about my strained relationship with Wesley.

"I'm telling you, Maya, I was too damn outdone when that slut showed up and wrapped her arms around him like he was her boo." I unzipped my backpack and removed my copy of the script. I needed to review my lines before taking the stage.

"And Lori just started groping on him as if you weren't standing there talking to him?" Maya asked.

"Yup. She was very disrespectful and almost got her butt kicked."

"We should find her and beat her down," Maya suggested, fully willing to issue a well-deserved punishment.

"I'm not even going to trip about Wesley and his little tramp. If that's what he wants then he can have her."

"Has he tried to contact you?" Maya asked.

"I don't know and don't care," I said without any type of sorrow or sentiment toward him.

"I don't understand why one minute Wesley is stalking you, begging you to call him, and now he's acting like player of the year."

"Do you want to know the theory I've come up with?" I asked.

"Yeah, what?" Maya was eager to hear my thoughts.

"I think Lori is doing Wesley. Giving him every exclusive, if you know what I mean."

"You think she's been giving him the punany?"

"Yes. Why else would she be acting so boldly?" I asked, arguing my point.

"That's messed up. I hate girls like that. Girls who know that a guy has a girlfriend and yet they still try to steal him away."

"You know the thing that hurts the most about all of this?"

"No, what?"

"He led me to believe that he wasn't like other guys. He made me feel as if I was so special and we were perfect for each other. All the risks I took just to be with him because I didn't want him to feel as if I'd ever abandon him."

"You did the right thing, Keysha. He's the one who messed up and when he realizes it, he'll come to you with a major sob story about his mistake."

"Yeah, whatever," I replied, cringing at the thought of Wesley coming around me.

"Hey, you two. Why are you sitting all the way back here?" Antonio asked as he walked up the aisle toward us. I smiled at him because he was looking as handsome as ever.

"Girl talk," I answered him with a smile.

"Are you talking about me?" Antonio asked coyly.

"Maybe and maybe not." I purposely flirted with him.

"You know there is an old saying, Keysha," Maya whispered to me. "The best way to get over one guy is to get under another one." I turned my attention back to Maya, who had a naughty grin on her face.

"You are so bad," I said, laughing at the sexual undertone of what she'd just said.

"Mind if I sit over here with you guys?" Antonio sat down before we invited him to do so. However, I didn't mind one bit.

"So why haven't you called or sent me a text today?" Antonio asked me.

"I don't know. I didn't think about it." I really didn't

send it because I didn't want to seem like some desperate girl looking to sink her teeth into him at the first sign of hope. I wanted him to chase me a little and then see what happened from there.

"Oh, it's like that. You didn't think about me at all. Not one time today?" Antonio's ego was bruised.

"Hmm, this sounds like it's turning into a private conversation." Maya rose to her feet and gathered her belongings. Before stepping away she turned and met my gaze. "Okay, Keysha girl. Don't forget to go over your lines before you get up on the stage."

"I know my lines by heart," I answered, putting her questions to rest.

"So what did you think about that kiss?" Antonio asked, staring directly into my eyes. He smiled and then swept his tongue across his lips. I crossed my legs and folded my arms across my breasts.

"It was okay," I answered, not wanting to overinflate his ego.

"Just okay?" he asked.

"Mmm-hmm," I answered back.

"Keysha, you are lying. You know you felt something more."

"Oh, really? So you know all about girls and what they think and feel, right?"

"I'm not going to say all of that, but I do know that kiss was more than just a kiss. It was like eating a chocolate ice cream cone on a hot summer afternoon. Every lick was…well, you know what I'm trying to say."

I was speechless. I wanted him to continue expressing

himself, but I was still trying to get past the image of his tongue licking circles around a chocolate ice cream cone. It was difficult for me to not want to be his chocolate delight melting all over his fingers.

"So are we still going to say our lines and kiss like that again tonight?" Antonio asked. I found my tongue parting my sweet lips to moisten them.

"Yes." I laughed nervously.

"Good." He placed his hand on my knee and I swear I could feel the heat of his hand through the fabric of my jeans. I suddenly felt like a lioness, craving for her king to continue his mating session.

Antonio and I performed our scenes with very little direction. It seemed as if the love affair that was written down on the page had somehow manifested inside of Antonio and me. We were inextricably drawn to each other. An undeniable chemistry flowed between us. When it came time for us to kiss each other, we did, and it felt as if all of the breath in my body left me the moment our lips met.

The director of the play loved the chemistry Antonio and I had and encouraged us to bring even more passion to the characters we were portraying. Afterward, Antonio and I walked backstage so that Priscilla, Maya and a few others could perform their parts. As Priscilla moved past me she whispered, "You kiss like a slut."

I couldn't let that comment go. I'd grown weary of her snide remarks and I fully intended to nip the beef between us in the bud. I reached out for some of Priscilla's hair, but I wasn't close enough. Antonio held me back just in time.

Priscilla met my gaze and I could see the flames of defiance in her eyes.

"Hey, what are you doing?" Antonio asked.

"Did you hear what she said to me when she walked past?" I asked through gritted teeth.

"No."

"She basically called me a whore and I'm going to straighten her ass out," I said, eager to walk onto the stage for a good old-fashioned catfight.

"Don't pay any attention to Priscilla. You know she's just jealous of you. Besides, I don't like girls who fight. Especially not a girl who I want to be my woman." Antonio placed my chin on the rim of his forefinger and gently tilted my face upward so that I could gaze at him. The passion in his eyes was unmistakable. In fact it was overpowering, and I found myself completely surrendering to his will.

"Focus on me and not Priscilla," he whispered as he lightly stroked my cheeks. I wanted to snatch off every stitch of clothing he had on and kiss him everywhere. My lust for him was stronger than it had ever been for any boy and I wondered if my yearning for him could turn into love.

twenty

WESLEY

Lori and I hung out at Mr. Submarine until around 6:00 p.m. We talked about a lot of stuff that was going on in each other's lives. I told her about how crazy my mother was and how my father and I were closer than we'd ever been. We talked about the hope and uncertainty of getting into a good college. We discussed some of the bizarre habits of the faculty and a few of the wild rumors floating around about teachers who were secretly dating students. When we left, I walked her home, which was without question out of my way. However, Lori had worked on me and had gotten me to calm down a little, as well as help me understand her perspective. I didn't agree with a lot of her actions and behavior, but there was something about hearing the logic and thoughts that motivated her. Along the route to her dad's house, there was a park. Lori, who was clearly in no hurry to return, suggested we stop and sit on the park bench for a little while longer. I agreed and a short time later, I found myself watching the bright sun duck down below the orange-and-red horizon.

Lori began stroking my hair. "You have very soft hair," Lori said, complimenting me on my finer grade of hair.

"Why are girls so big on hair?" I asked even though I sort of already knew the answer to that question.

"Our hair or guys' hair?" she asked for clarification.

"Guys' hair. I mean, dudes don't care much about hair outside of getting a fresh cut. We don't care about what shampoo or conditioner goes into it. We just wash it, and move on."

"Girls look for men with a finer grade of hair to determine if they want to have a baby with the guy. No girl wants to give birth to a nappy-headed baby or at least that's been sort of the unwritten rule and tradition."

"What's wrong with nappy hair?" I pressed the issue even though I didn't particularly care one way or the other.

"Nothing really. It's just a hang-up some people have. That's one of the reasons I like India.Arie's song, 'I Am Not My Hair.'"

"Yeah, that's a cut," I admitted as the tune began to play inside my mind.

"So, Wesley…truthfully. What's the deal with you and Keysha? Are you guys still dating or what?"

I shrugged. "I don't know where Keysha and I are. And honestly, you being here in Illinois isn't helping me win any redemption points with her."

"If she truly wanted to be with you she would have called or at a minimum sent you a text by now. Has she done that?" Lori asked, prying heavily into my relationship with Keysha. I removed my cell phone to see if I'd missed any messages from Keysha. To my disappointment she had not tried to contact me at all.

"No. She hasn't tried to reach me."

Lori traced the outline of my face with her index finger. "I don't want to sound insensitive, but it's over between you and her whether you realize it or not."

"I keep feeling like if I could just get her to listen to me, she'll come around. We'll forgive each other, renew our commitment to one another and move forward."

"You know what you need to do?" Lori asked.

"What?"

"You need to stop pining over her. No girl wants a sappy, needy guy," Lori professed.

I frowned at her comment. "I'm not a sappy guy," I said, shooting down her perception of me.

"Oh, yes, you are." Lori chuckled. "You're kind of a hopeless romantic who doesn't realize that the love story express has derailed."

"That is so cold." I felt as if she was stepping on my heart.

"What's so cold about the truth? I mean if more people would be truthful with each other we would have a lot less misunderstandings."

"So what's the real truth about you, Lori? Why are you in my life?"

"I've told you a thousand times. I believe destiny is guiding us toward each other."

I laughed; she didn't see her own hypocrisy. "And you call me the hopeless romantic."

"Oh, you're trying to bust me out now?"

"Why beat around the bush?" I asked.

"True. Why should I beat around the bush? Do you remember the first day we met at your grandmother's house?" Lori stood up to face me and then straddled me. She then positioned herself so that her behind was resting on my lap. I instinctively wrapped my arm around her waist.

"Yeah, I remember," I said, inconspicuously guiding my hand around the curve of her hip.

"I knew I liked you right away. You didn't have to say a single word to me. There was something about you that I was drawn to. I was drawn to you in a way that I'd never experienced before. Now tell me the truth—when you saw me, weren't you attracted to me?"

I thought about what she'd just said and tried to think clearly instead of allowing my lust to offer up a false answer.

"When I saw you I thought you were decent-looking. I sized you up and made some assumptions."

"You're beating around the bush, Wesley." Lori craned her neck toward me and kissed me. The fluctuation of Lori's hips against my body during the kiss shifted my thinking. I suddenly yearned and ached for her. I wanted to explore every inch of her and learn the secrets and mysteries of her body, which had not been discovered by a man. "Did you want to have sex with me when you first saw me?" Lori boldly asked.

"Yes," I answered as she sucked on my bottom lip.

"Then you are destined to unlock my treasure and enjoy the fortune that awaits you inside of me."

* * *

By the time I arrived home it was close to eight in the evening. I was thankful neither my dad nor grandmother were there to ask a bunch of questions that I didn't feel like answering. I went to my room, undressed and took a long shower. When I was done, I put on some sweatpants and my Thornwood T-shirt. I went to my room, rested on my bed, and replayed what had taken place between Lori and me. Admittedly, I was confused. My lust dominated and tortured my devotion to Keysha. I grabbed my cell phone from the nightstand and sent a text message to Keysha.

Wesley: Hey U.

To my complete surprise and utter shock she returned my text.

Keysha: Hey U back.

Wesley: What R U doing?

Keysha: Wuz talking 2 Mike. Now N my room doing homework.

Wesley: R U mad @ me?

Keysha: I wuz but not anymore. U have a new girl. I'm over it. I have moved on.

Wesley: It's not like that.

Keysha: Yeah right. I am not stupid.

Wesley: I didn't say u were.

Keysha: QQ.

Wesley: Shoot.

Keysha: Y is Lori at Thornwood?

Wesley: She had to leave after her house got shot up.

Keysha: What????

Wesley: Some gangbangers shot up her house b-cause she was a witness.

Keysha: Witness 2 what?

Wesley: Her boyfriend shot me.

Keysha: WTF?

Wesley: I no. It's complicated.

Keysha: Sounds like u have a mess on ur hands. So now U R in 2 gangster girls?

Wesley: Y R U trip n? U should trust me.

Keysha: I did and U broke my heart. Can't let dat happen again.

Welsey: I'm sorry. I really am.

Keysha: It is what it is.

Wesley: I want 2 C U again.

Keysha: 4 what?

Wesley: b-cause

Keysha: Nope. All U R gonna do is play me.

Wesley: U don't believe dat.

Keysha: QQ.

Wesley: Shoot.

Keysha: is she giving u the punany?

Wesley: No.

Keysha: Yeah right. I bet she want 2.

Wesley: QQ.

Keysha: O now U got questions.

Wesley: Yes. Do U love me?

Keysha: In what way?

Wesley: The same way U did when i left.

Keysha: QQ.

Wesley: How R U gonna answer a Q with a Q?

Keysha: Do she love u?

Wesley: In what way?

Keysha: WTF Wesley? Answer the damn Q.

Wesley: What do U want me 2 say?

Keysha: How about the truth?

Wesley: Y R we talking about her? We should talk about us.

Keysha: QQ.

Wesley: What?

Keysha: Y did U let her interrupt us at my locker?

Wesley: I was surprised 2 C her. I didn't know she was here.

Keysha: U R lying 2 me.

Wesley: No I am not.

Keysha: Yeah right.

Wesley: QQ.

Keysha: What?

Wesley: When can I C U again?

Keysha: I don't have time 2 C U.

Wesley: Y not?

Keysha: I have practice.

Wesley: 4 what?

Keysha: I made the drama club. Got the lead part.

Wesley: Really? Congrats. Did not no dat. Can't wait 2 C it.

Keysha: QQ.

Wesley: Yeah?

Keysha: How is ur shoulder?

Wesley: Good getting better every day. I C a doctor later in da week.

Keysha: So do I.

Wesley: Y what's wrong?

Keysha: Folks R making me C a shrink b-cause of U.

Wesley: Huh?

Keysha: I ran away from home 2 C U and U had dat be-huch there kissing all over U and U made me feel really stupid.

Wesley: I did not no U ran away from home 2 C me.

Keysha: Dat is how deeply I used 2 love U. Now I got 2 C a damn shrink b-cause my folks think I am crazy and bipolar.

Wesley: I'm sorry. I did not no.

Keysha: Well now u do. I told my dad our love wuz 2 strong 2 B broken.

Wesley: I still do love U Keysha.

Keysha: Ne-grow please! I heard dat u wuz @ Mr. Submarine getting a rub down!

Wesley: What U got spies now?

Keysha: Well iz it true?

Wesley: QQ.

Keysha: What?

Wesley: Can we just start over?

Keysha: I already have. TTYL.

twenty-one

KEYSHA

OVer the next several weeks I focused on school, and concentrated on my homework and my ever-evolving relationship with Antonio. During this same time period my general disgruntlement with Priscilla Grisby continued to grow. On numerous occasions her snide remarks, piss-poor attitude and general dislike of me warranted a good old-fashioned butt-whipping. However, I held back because I was truly trying to be a bigger person than her and didn't want to be reduced to her level by getting into a scuffle.

Wesley continually stalked me via text messages, phone calls and unwelcome visits to my locker. Oddly enough, he never showed up when Antonio was visiting me. He always managed to come at a time when Antonio wasn't around. I wasn't sure if it was purely coincidence or if Wesley had somehow timed his visits. He unyieldingly tried to get me to agree to date him again. I'll admit that somewhere in my heart there was still a place for him, but I just wasn't willing to allow my heart to be bruised by him again.

"Wesley. We'll always be friends," I told him one day when he was trying particularly hard to win back my affections.

"But I want to be more than just friends. Can't you see how sorry I am and how hard I'm trying to win you back?"

"Wesley, you really need to stop doing this. You're starting to get really creepy," I said, hoping to get him to back off a little.

"Oh, now I'm creepy?" I'd insulted him as well as hurt his feelings.

"Not in a bad way. Just in an 'I'm concerned' sort of way." I tried to clean up my comment to protect his feelings. I don't know why; I guess I just felt sorry deep inside. Besides, I could tell he was truly struggling with accepting the reality that he'd lost me.

"So are you saying that after all we've been through it's totally over?"

"It's decision time for you, Wesley. You can continue to come around begging me to date you again and keep on getting your feelings hurt. Or we can just be friends and leave it at that," I explained to him the best way I knew how.

"You still want me. I know you do. I'm not giving up on us, Keysha." Wesley frightened me with his response. The phone calls, texts and visits to my locker did not stop. I saw a darker part of him that I'd never seen before.

My relationship with Antonio continued to blossom due to the fact we were spending a large amount of time together working on the play. I enjoyed my interactions with him. As I got to know him, I learned of his ambitions and life goals. He wanted to attend a performing arts school and one day become an actor like Denzel Washington, Al Pacino and Jamie Foxx.

"Those are my favorite male actors," he said to me one Saturday evening when he and I were out on a date. We'd stopped for a bite to eat at a restaurant after seeing a local production of *From the Mississippi Delta* at the ETA Creative Arts Theater. We enjoyed the play tremendously. It was about a woman living in a time and a world that denied her the most basic rights. So she journeyed from Mississippi to Chicago and through her journey she gained the strength to appreciate herself not only as a woman, but also as an individual. Antonio and I talked about the play at great length, but then we began discussing some of his favorite actors.

"Jamie Foxx has so many amazing talents. He can sing, play the piano and act. Plus, dude is ripped in the muscle department."

"I will give you that. Jamie Foxx is nice-looking," I agreed with him as I took a sip of my iced tea.

"Anyway, I know it's going to be very hard, but once I break in to acting I want to take on roles that challenge me and push me to my limit."

"Push you to your limit how?" I inquired.

"Have you ever seen the movie *Cast Away* with Tom Hanks?" Antonio asked.

"Is that the movie where his plane crashed on an island?" I hoped I'd recalled the right film.

"Yes. And the only thing he had to act with was a

freaking volleyball he named Wilson. It is nothing short of amazing the way he carried that entire film. He did it all through body language and narration."

"I didn't realize you were so passionate about acting," I said, pleasantly surprised. He was most certainly different from any guy I'd ever dated.

"It's not just acting. It's about the performing arts as a whole," Antonio said, making gestures with his hands.

"So where does all of your passion come from?" I asked just as our waitress set the food we'd ordered before us. I'd ordered a turkey club sandwich and Antonio had ordered spicy buffalo wings. I immediately started eating, but Antonio bowed his head and said a quick prayer. I stopped eating until he was done.

"My parents were both in theater. My mom used to be an Alvin Ailey dancer before she got arthritis, which has slowed her down considerably. My father is a director at the Goodman Theater downtown."

"How come you never told me any of this?" I was disappointed about not knowing this.

"I don't like to talk about it because then people may get the impression that the school is playing favoritism by giving me lead parts in the school play," he answered as he dabbed the corners of his mouth for buffalo sauce trapped there from his wings.

"I've never been to a professional stage play before," I admitted.

"Really? Oh, wow. They are so much fun. In fact, I should take you to see the Blue Man Group. It's playing at one of the theaters in the city."

"I've seen the commercials for that production. It looks so exciting," I said, feeling giddy at the idea of going places I'd never even considered.

"I've seen it before. You'd love it, Keysha. I just know you would. But you know what is truly amazing to me?"

"No. What?" I asked.

"You."

"Me?" I laughed. "What's so amazing about me?"

"Growing up, my parents were always taking me to some production. And I've seen my fair share of good actors and bad ones. For you to have no formal training and be as good as you are is a gift. You should seriously consider learning all that you can about the craft. I can see your name on the movie billboard—*The Drama in Her Life,* starring Keysha Kendall." I laughed, but somewhere deep inside of me, I liked the sound of it.

When Antonio dropped me off after dinner he pulled into the driveway and got out of the car. He opened up the car door for me.

"It's okay. I can let myself in," I said teasingly.

"Nope. Your dad really grilled me when I came to pick you up, so I want to make sure he knows that I've returned you home safe and sound."

"You really don't have to do that. Jordan is very over-protective of me," I said, feeling somewhat embarrassed. No sooner had I said that than the floodlights came on and Jordan unlocked the door.

"Hello, sir," Antonio greeted him right away.

"Antonio." Jordan eyed him suspiciously.

"I just wanted to let you know that I've returned Keysha home. Safe and sound." Antonio grinned.

Jordan hesitated, but then smiled and said, "Thank you."

"I'll see you later," Antonio said to me as he walked back to his car. As I stepped inside I became irritated because I didn't get a good-night kiss.

The night of the show had finally arrived and I was a nervous wreck. I stood in front of my bathroom mirror and kept going over and over my lines in my head, making sure I hadn't had some type of bizarre memory lapse. Just as I was finishing up in the bathroom I heard a knock at the door.

"Mike, leave me alone," I shouted through the door.

"It's not Mike, honey." I heard the voice of Grandmother Katie and immediately flung the door open.

"What are you doing here?" I asked as I hugged her. I inhaled her sweet-scented perfume as she embraced me tightly.

"You knew I couldn't let you have your very first stage performance and not be there. Come on. You know me better than that." She smiled at me.

"I'm so happy to see you, but I'm also so unbelievably nervous. My stomach is doing all sorts of weird things."

"You just have a case of the jitters, that's all. Every performer gets them, but the moment you step out onto the stage and the lights come up, amazingly that panicky feeling vanishes into thin air."

"I hope you're right because right now I feel like I don't even know my own name."

"You'll be just fine, honey. I'll be sitting out there in the audience watching you and cheering you on." Grand-mother Katie stepped back to take a good look at me. "My grandbaby. An Oscar-winning actress."

"I don't know about all of that." I laughed nervously.

"You just never know what life has in store for you," she said as Barbara came up the stairs behind her.

"How are you doing, Keysha?" she asked.

"Okay," I answered.

"Are you just about ready for me to drive you up to the school?" Barbara asked.

"Yeah. Just let me grab my purse from my bedroom and I'll be right down. Oh, do you have your tickets?" I inquired, wanting to be sure that I'd given them to her.

"Yes, I've got them."

"Be sure to sit in the center seats so you'll be able to see everything," I reminded her.

When I walked downstairs and into the family room, Jordan, Mike and Sabrina were there to wish me luck and offer me their support. I hugged them all before leaving with Barbara.

"Maya, I can't believe this night has actually arrived," I said, taking her hand into my own. I squeezed it to show her just how intensely excited I was.

"I know. I'm feeling nervous as well, but we're going to knock them dead," she assured me.

Maya and I walked backstage, where there was a flurry of activity. The stage crew was making final adjustments to the set. Folks were buzzing around looking for their costumes and trying to find someone to help them put on their makeup. Maya led me into our dressing room, where I sat down, took a few deep breaths and began to prepare. An hour later, I was in full costume and standing backstage peering out into the theater, which was filling up very rapidly.

"You shouldn't peep out at the audience." Antonio came up from behind and startled me.

"Jeez, you scared the crap out of me!" I said as I placed one hand over my heart.

"Sorry, I didn't mean to do that," he apologized as I adjusted his wardrobe.

"You look magnificent, baby," I said as I gave him a peck on the cheek.

"Hey, you two, everyone is looking for you down in the casting room," Maya said as she approached.

Antonio and I went into the casting room for some last-minute instructions before the show. A short while later I was sitting on the sofa, cloaked from view by the giant black stage curtains. I clenched my fists a few times in an effort to calm my nerves. I heard the announcer welcome our guests to the show and finally, the curtains were drawn back and the audience began clapping. The opening scene went off without a hitch. The audience laughed at the funny parts and everyone remembered their lines. During the second scene one of the cast members, whose part was to behave like an over-the-top disc jockey, lost his wig. However, he made light of it by picking it up, putting it back on lopsided and continuing on. The audience loved it. When Antonio and I kissed each other there was a loud chorus of oohs and aahs from the spectators.

When the show concluded, everyone was called out

onto the stage by name. When my name was called, I heard Jordan's voice roar above everyone else's. I looked up into the crowded stands and saw him, Barbara, Grandmother Katie, Mike and Sabrina all waving at me. My heart was filled with so much happiness and I was so overcome with joy that I started crying. I couldn't help it. I'd never achieved anything like this in my entire life and it was a very defining moment of sorts. The clapping and the cheering continued as the curtains were drawn to a close. As soon as we were all hidden from sight, our voices erupted in jubilation. All of the actors and actresses formed a giant circle and began jumping around. Even Priscilla was happy about the performance and didn't give me any grief.

The cast came out into the hallway to meet parents, guests and friends who'd come out. Jordan gave me flowers and each member of my family gave me a big hug. Others who were there congratulated me and expressed how pleased they were with my performance. As I was mingling with the mob of people gathered in the hallway, I felt someone tap me on the shoulder. When I turned around I saw Wesley. I was so excited that I gave him a giant hug and a kiss on the cheek. In doing so I inhaled the unmistakable scent of alcohol. I wrinkled my nose and turned my head in the opposite direction.

"You were incredible, Keysha!" Wesley congratulated me.

"Thank you," I said, turning back and looking into his eyes, which appeared to be glassed over.

"How have you been?" he asked.

"Good," I answered as someone passing by gave me the thumbs-up for my performance. I smiled at them and then turned my attention back to Wesley.

"I know this is probably not a very good time to ask, but I was wondering if you had a date for the—"

"Keysha." I turned around and saw Antonio approaching me with his mom and dad.

"Antonio," I called out and hugged him.

"This is my mom, Leslie, and this is my dad, Ray." I gave both of them a hug and thanked them for coming.

"You guys did a spectacular job," said Antonio's father, who was clearly very proud of him.

"Before I forget, I want to ask you something," Antonio said and took my hands into his.

"What?" I smiled at him so hard my cheeks ached.

"Will you go to prom with me?"

"Wait, what did he just ask you?" Wesley interrupted. I looked at Wesley and then back at Antonio. I hesitated because I felt sort of odd. But I wasn't about to let Wesley ruin my moment.

"Keysha, you're supposed to say—"

"Yes, Antonio. I'd be happy to go to prom with you," I said.

"Get away from my girl!" Wesley growled like a wounded wolf. In his rage he swung his fist, intending to hit Antonio, but since his right arm was still in a sling and he was intoxicated, he only succeeded in knocking himself off balance and tumbling to the floor.

twenty-two

WESLEY

when I awoke the following morning, I had a massive headache, which was without question due to a hangover. I barely remember coming into the house and getting in my bed. I do remember tumbling over the garden hose, which I'd forgotten to coil back up onto its spindle.

I groaned as I turned my back toward the window because the sunlight coming in was too bright. I rubbed my forehead with the palm of my hand, hoping and praying it would make my head stop hurting. I glanced at my cell phone, which had fallen to the floor. I reached out, picked it up and noticed I had a text message.

Keysha: I'm worried about you. Call me.

"Yeah, right," I grumbled as I set the phone on a nearby nightstand. "You don't care about me, Keysha. If you did, you would've given me another chance. You knew how much I needed you, yet you turned your back on me. Go to hell!"

I needed aspirin because rubbing my forehead wasn't cutting it. I pulled myself to an upright position and sat on the edge of the bed. I felt a little light-headed. After I collected myself, I grabbed my cell phone and walked down the hall toward the bathroom. I opened the medicine cabinet and removed a bottle of extra strength Tylenol. I filled a Dixie cup with water then swallowed two pills. I closed the lid on the toilet, sat down and then rested my elbows on my knees. I slumped my head between my shoulders and meditated on my life.

I was happy I'd gotten in the house before my dad, who'd finally returned to work. He stayed out late in order to attend a welcome-back party his coworkers hosted in his honor. Grandmother Lorraine returned home once she'd received word from her neighbor that the young men who'd wrecked my dad's car and shot up Lori's grandmother's house had been arrested for trying to rob a local convenience store.

I scored some alcohol from my old drinking buddy Ed Daley, who'd recently returned to Thornwood from rehab, which obviously didn't work out for him. Ed was more than happy to supply me with alcohol so that he could restore the tradition of calling me Whiskey Wesley. I can't pinpoint exactly when I made the decision to back-pedal and allow myself to be seduced by the false promise of alcohol. I suppose I was searching for someone to blame for my misery. One day I was sitting around de-pressed about how everything had turned out: the house fire, the move to Indianapolis, being shot, the loss of the court case, the loss of Keysha and my vexing relationship with Lori. I was in pain and my world was a spinning blur of drama and heartache. Alcohol offered a way to numb my feelings and slow everything down.

My cell phone vibrated again. I looked at it and saw Ed Daley had sent me a text message.

Ed: U got a prom date yet? If so I've scored a hotel room 4 some after prom action.

Good old Ed, I thought. He always knew how to pull strings and get people to do favors for him. I exhaled and stammered for a moment before deciding to give Lori a jingle. When she answered the phone she sounded as if she was around a crowd of people.

"Hey, stranger," she greeted.

"Where are you?" I asked, wishing the Tylenol would kick in.

"At the Cricket Store looking at cell phones. What's up?"

"So are we going to do this prom thing or what?" I got straight to the point.

"You can't ask me any better than that? And why are you talking so slowly? You sound like you're high or something."

"I just woke up and I'm still a little groggy."

"You just woke up? Wesley, it's noon."

"Really? I didn't realize it was so late in the day."

"You don't sound as if you really want to go to prom with me. You've been ignoring me. I thought you were trying to hook back up with your beloved Keysha. What happened with that?" Lori was being her usual feisty self. She knew damn well she wanted to go, but was making this more difficult than it had to be.

"I don't want to talk about Keysha. She's old news as far as I'm concerned."

"Oh, really?" I could picture Lori's cynical smile in my mind.

"Lori, will you please go to junior prom with me?" I asked as politely as I could so that I could get her answer and hit Ed back.

"Yes. I'd love to go to prom with you. Get dressed. I'll be over in about thirty minutes. I have my mom's car for a few hours. I'll come by, scoop you up and we'll go look at prom dresses." I could tell that I'd clearly just made her day. I really didn't feel like shopping for prom dresses, but I didn't have anything else to do.

"Okay," I agreed and ended the call. I sent Ed a text back informing him that I did have a date.

The following week I was given a clean bill of health and no longer needed the use of the sling. It was liberating to have the use of my right arm again. I no longer had to ask Lori to write my notes for me, nor did I have to worry about forcing my left hand to do tasks it wasn't accustomed to doing.

It was now Wednesday and I'd just entered the gymnasium. I was taking a shortcut and was on my way to the cafeteria. I wasn't even paying attention to the two girls trotting around the track until one of them called me. I looked up and saw Keysha and her girlfriend Maya.

"Hey, you," Keysha said and continued to jog in place.

Her skin was glistening with perspiration and her breathing was labored.

"What's up?" I acted nonchalant, as if her stopping to speak with me didn't matter to me one way or another.

"How have you been?" She stopped jogging in place.

"I'll catch up with you later, Keysha," Maya said as she nodded her head in my direction.

"Okay, Maya. I'll see you in the locker room in a minute," Keysha said as Maya continued on.

"When did you start running?" I asked. Ever since Keysha got involved with the theater people she'd become a different person.

"Maya convinced me to do it. We're working on shedding a few pounds for the prom."

"Yeah, the prom. You're going with that player, Antonio the sex machine." I didn't hold back the way I felt about him at all.

"Antonio is not like that, Wesley." Keysha was defending him and I didn't like it.

"Yeah, right. Whatever, Keysha, I've got to go," I said and began to walk away.

"Wesley, wait. I want us to be friends. I don't want any hard feelings between us," she said. I didn't like her anymore and I damn sure didn't want to be her friend.

"I don't want to be your friend. What did you tell me a few weeks back? Oh, yeah, it's decision time. And I've decided that I don't want to have anything to do with a girl who doesn't believe a person can make a mistake. I don't want to be friends with a girl who is suspicious and I damn sure don't want to be friends with you," I snapped.

"You know you don't mean that, Wesley. I know you better than you think I do."

"You don't know me, Keysha." I dismissed her claim as hogwash.

"You're depressed, Wesley. That's why you've started drinking again."

"And you're crazy, Keysha. That's why you're seeing a shrink!" I yelled at her. My animosity toward her had grown into raging hatred. I glared into her eyes so she could see the heat in my eyes.

"Yo, Wesley. Come here." I turned in the direction of the voice. At the other end of the gym Ed Daley was waving me over.

"Wesley, Ed is bad news. You shouldn't—"

"Keysha, stay out of my business!" I growled before turning my back and walking away.

twenty-three

KEYSHA

when I went into the locker room to freshen up and change clothes, Maya was exiting the shower. She had a towel wrapped around her body and another one around her wet hair.

"What was that all about?" she asked as I got undressed.

"Just trying to be friendly, that's all," I answered as I replayed in my mind how mean Wesley was to me.

"I can understand that. Whenever I break up with a guy, I like to try and remain friends," Maya agreed.

"Maya." I paused and collected my thoughts. "Do you think I did the right thing by breaking up with Wesley? I mean, he seems to be lost these days and I can't help but feel as if I'm to blame."

"Keysha, are you kidding me? Please don't tell me you've allowed Whiskey Wesley to place a guilt trip on you." I didn't like the fact that Maya referred to him as "Whiskey Wesley," but I didn't correct her.

"No, I don't feel guilty. I'm just worried about him. I want Wesley to be happy."

"Okay, first of all, let's go over the facts. Did Wesley get shot over a girl?"

"Yes," I answered

"When you moved heaven and earth to go see him did he have a girl in his room who'd been kissing all over him?"

"Yes," I answered.

"When he came back home, did his girlfriend from Indianapolis mysteriously and ironically show up and now lives near Wesley?"

"Okay, Maya, I see your point."

"He dogged you, Keysha. You were totally faithful to him and he tried to play you. There is no way I could feel sorry for a guy who treated me like crap." Maya was brazen with her criticism of Wesley.

"I know all of those things are true, but for some reason I still care about him," I admitted.

"You'll get over it. Trust me. I've seen my fair share of boyfriends and the way you're feeling now will fade. Besides, you have fine-ass Antonio to help you get over Wesley," Maya reminded me. I laughed.

"Antonio is super fine!" I chuckled before stepping away to take a shower.

That weekend Maya made arrangements to get the keys to her mom's car and she and I scheduled an appointment at Planned Parenthood health clinic so that I could get some form of birth control. I honestly didn't think I'd ever take her up on her earlier offer, but my relationship with

Antonio was passionate and I knew it was only a matter of time before I was going to completely lose it, pin him down and do everything imaginable to him. Maya was a regular at Planned Parenthood but she didn't want her mom to know that she was sexually active and Lord knows I didn't want Barbara or Jordan to know all of my business.

My appointment went well and I got the birth control patch. It cost me a small fortune to get it, but I felt it was well worth the effort and expense. Afterward Maya dropped me back off at home she then had to rush off because her mom needed the car.

As soon as I walked in the house, Barbara asked if I wanted to hang out with her. "I'm going to run some errands. When I'm finished we can go shopping for a prom dress."

"Yes," I said jubilantly. "Let me run upstairs and get my magazines that have some styles I'm looking for."

"Okay. I'm going to pull the car out of the garage."

I ran back inside the house, scooped up my publications and rushed back out the door. Barbara and I ended up spending the remainder of the weekend on a hunt for the perfect dress. Admittedly, we both agreed that we waited a little too late to shop for a dress because most everything had been picked over. Barbara and I were on a straight-up mission to find the perfect dress, shoes and accessories. We had a few sticking points because our tastes and styles were different. Barbara was the classic conservative type and I wanted to let it all hang out, especially since I'd dropped a few pounds and had more curves for Antonio to enjoy.

I was so ecstatic about my dress that I called Maya as soon as I got in the house. "Maya, you are going to flip out when you see the Jovani prom dress I've picked out. We've got to get our exercise routine into high gear because I'll be showing a lot of skin."

"Ooh, I can't wait to see this dress, Keysha." Maya was brimming with an equal amount of excitement. "I hope you don't think you're the only one who's going to be showing some skin. I've got a hot dress, too."

"What color is your dress?" I asked, hoping we wouldn't end up at prom looking like twins.

"Turquoise," Maya answered. "And yours?"

"Yellow." I sighed, fully relieved. "The dress is strapless and the back is cutout. I'm going to look so damn hot in this dress," I said as I looked at the dress, which was hanging on the inside of my closet door.

"Okay, when can I see it?" Maya asked.

"Girl, you can come on over right now," I said. "Oh, and the shoes… Whew! Those are smoking."

"How much did you spend?" Maya inquired.

"I didn't spend anything. That is why I love my stepmom." I laughed. "The dress cost over three hundred and the shoes were another two hundred."

"Okay. I've got to see what you bought. I can't go to prom and look like the maid standing next to you. I'll bring my dress over so you can see it. Let me see if I can get the car from my mom. When I get it, I'll be right over."

Prom night had finally arrived and I was both excited and tired. Excited because of all the fanfare and pageantry surrounding such an event. Tired because I'd spent most of the night sleeping in an upright position; I didn't want to mess up my hair. I wanted it to look perfect. Grandmother Katie drove back to see me and take photos. As always, it was great to see her smiling round face and receive her warm hugs. I'd gone on a serious diet and workout program during the time leading up to prom. Mike even showed me how to lift weights properly and for the first time in my life my arms looked toned and muscular.

"Keysha, Antonio is here," Mike hollered up the stairwell. Grandmother Katie and Barbara were both working feverishly to make sure the fabric was snug enough to hold my boobs in place and that my hair and makeup was flawless. I put in my earrings and looked at myself in the mirror.

"I barely recognize myself," I said, feeling overwhelmed with emotion.

"Don't cry now," Grandmother Katie said. "You'll smudge your makeup if you do."

"Okay," I said, taking in a few deep breaths to quiet my nervousness.

"Oh, you look like a princess," Barbara said as she stepped back and took a good look at me.

"Do you really think so?" I asked. Grandmother Katie made one final adjustment to my clothing.

"Okay, we're going to go downstairs and take your picture when you come down the stairs."

"Okay." I smiled then laughed nervously. A few moments later, I heard Grandmother Katie telling Antonio how handsome he looked.

"Okay, Keysha. Come on down." I began slowly walking down the stairs as if I was a princess or a Hollywood movie star. When I caught my first glimpse of Antonio, he looked absolutely princely in his black tuxedo. His hair was freshly cut and he was holding a wrist corsage. The way the expression changed on his face when our eyes met was priceless. My entire body was tingling with nervous energy. I glanced over at Jordan, who had a look of shock and awe blanketing his face. Then slowly, like the rising of the morning sun, a proud smile spread across his face. Mike gave me the thumbs-up and then began taking pictures with his camera phone. Jordan hugged me and told me how stunning I looked. Antonio approached me and placed the corsage on my wrist and then placed a light kiss on my cheek.

"You look amazing," he whispered.

"Ahem." Jordan cleared his throat loudly and then boldly proclaimed, "You know that you're not getting any, right?"

"Jordan!" Grandmother Katie looked at him.

"What? I'm just letting the boy know what time it is," Jordan said, defending himself while Grandmother Katie glared at him.

Antonio and I took several photos in the house and outside. Several neighbors who were out walking their dogs or doing spring yard work took time to compliment us on how gorgeous we looked. Jordan insisted on renting a limousine for us and from what Barbara told me, he tipped the driver handsomely to ensure that we had a wonderful time.

After having the limousine driver take us by Antonio's

house for photos and then to Maya's house for additional pictures, we were finally on our way to prom, which was being held at the Hyatt Hotel at the McCormick Place Convention Center. Antonio and I entered the grand ballroom as if we were the king and queen of the world and were madly in love with each other. I was irresistible and Antonio couldn't keep his hands off me. Not that I really minded; I'd already made up my mind to sleep with him. Misalo's older brother rented a huge hotel suite for us. From what I understood, there were two bedrooms in the suite. One for Antonio and me, and one for Maya and Misalo.

The music was hot and a number of friends from the drama club came over to chat it up with us. Antonio and I didn't dance until a slow song came on. It was "I Stay in Love" by Mariah Carey. Antonio and I swayed to the music, got lost in each other's eyes and kissed. I sang to him, hoping he could see all of my intentions and yet be sensitive enough to understand how fragile and delicate my heart was.

The DJ switched up the music and began playing a song called "Birthday Sex" by Jeremih. The crowd went wild and began to sing out the chorus in unison.

Following that the DJ played a slew of popular dance songs, and the crowd got even louder. When the DJ finally put on a slow song, I grabbed Maya, who was dancing next to us with Misalo, and said, "Come to the bathroom with me. I am so hot now." Maya agreed and we both stepped away from our men. As we walked down a hotel corridor I saw Wesley standing near a water fountain.

"Wesley," I called to him as I approached. When he

looked at me his eyes were bloodred and the pungent odor of alcohol choked the air around us.

"Damn, you look good. You look a hundred times better than Lori, but I ain't gonna tell her that." Wesley leaned back against the wall.

"That's a mean thing to say, Wesley," I scolded him.

"Whatever, trick!" Wesley looked at me as if he hated the day I was born.

"You need help, Wesley."

"The only thing I need is a damn drink." Wesley's words were slow and measured.

"Whatever, Wesley," I said and entered the bathroom. I refused to let him ruin such a perfect night.

twenty-four

WESLEY

"I saw you talking to Keysha. She's lucky she left before I got over here. Are you still licking your wounds over that bitch?" Lori had been drinking with me and she couldn't hold her liquor or her tongue as well as I could.

"No," I answered, rolling my eyes and grumbling at the same time.

"Good, because all the woman you need is standing right in front of you," Lori reminded me. We kissed each other and I allowed my hands to enjoy the swell of her butt.

"Come on, let's go. I'm ready to do you," Lori said. "I'm going to screw Keysha out of your system. You said that Ed got us a hotel room, right?"

"Yeah, the Ramada Inn on Forty-seventh Street and Lake Shore Drive. He's already given me the spare key." I removed the room key and showed it to her.

"Well, come on then. Let's make this happen." Lori and

I staggered out of the hotel and into the parking garage, where her mom's car was parked.

"Give me the keys. I'll drive," I said because I knew I was much more alert than she was.

"Boy, please. I'm not going to let you drive my mother's car. I got it," she assured me.

Once inside the car, we made out. We explored each other before she finally pulled away and adjusted her clothes.

"Is the bottle of rum still in here?" I asked.

"Here you go," Lori stated smugly as she pulled the large liquor bottle from underneath the driver's seat. She unscrewed the top and shakily poured the amber-colored liquid in the empty plastic cups sitting in the console.

"Whoa, hold up." I grabbed the bottle from her when I noticed she had overfilled the cups. "You're wasting it." I took the cap and screwed it back on the bottle, then put it under my seat.

"Please." Lori rolled her eyes. "I didn't spill that much." She picked up one of the cups, and took a healthy sip before handing it over to me.

I really needed to get my head right before we headed to the hotel. My mind was a jumbled mess since my breakup with Keysha. I quickly poured the rum down my throat and felt my insides heat up. All at once I felt completely mellow and lay my head back against the headrest. A feeling of drowsiness washed over me, and I felt myself succumbing to darkness.

twenty-five

KEYSHA

when Maya and I returned to the ballroom, off in the distance on the other side of the room I saw Priscilla talking to Antonio.

"Why is that tramp trying to get all up on Antonio?" I asked Maya as I quickened my pace.

"I don't know, but I heard that she couldn't get a date and came here with some of her girlfriends," Maya explained.

"Come on," I said and we maneuvered through the crowd toward him.

"That is so damn tacky!" I said, purposefully in Maya's ear over the loud bass of the music.

"I would agree," Maya said.

"Hey, baby." I greeted Antonio with an embrace. I looped my arm around him and stood at his side, glaring at Priscilla, whose makeup was streaking down her cheeks. It was clear that she was crying.

"I really need to speak to you, Antonio!" Priscilla shouted.

"We don't have anything to talk about. I've told you, girl. Leave me alone," Antonio fired back at her.

"Yeah, leave him alone and go get your own man!" I wrinkled my eyebrows and stepped in front of Antonio, ready to deal with Priscilla once and for all.

"How could you be so cold, Antonio? I'm pregnant with your baby!" Priscilla screamed loud and clear. I felt as if I'd just been kicked in the gut.

A hush of shocked silence fell over the crowd, and it seemed everyone was staring at me. Antonio just stood there with his hands in his pants pockets, unsure of what to say. Priscilla gave me a venomous look. "Yeah, that's right. I'm pregnant with his baby!"

The whole scenario was totally mortifying, and a feeling of claustrophobia came over me. I raced for the exit doors before the tears of humiliation could run down my cheeks. "This is so embarrassing. Why do I have the worst luck with guys?" I cried as I raced as fast as I could down the empty hallway.

QUESTIONS FOR DISCUSSION

1. Wesley doesn't particularly care for Lori, yet in her time of need he comes to her rescue. Explain why you feel Wesley got involved instead of allowing Lori and Percy to deal with their rocky relationship issues.

2. Do you think Keysha was justified in going against her father's wishes and traveling to Indianapolis to see Wesley? Why or why not?

3. Wesley allowed Lori to manipulate him a lot throughout the story. Is it possible that Wesley secretly had a crush on Lori? Why or why not?

4. Both Lori and Wesley have to deal with being bullied by gang members. At one point Lori's house gets sprayed with bullets. What other options could Wesley have considered to avoid additional confrontations with Percy and his gang? Also, discuss some additional measures that can be taken to eliminate violence in your neighborhood or school.

5. Keysha demonstrated just how much she cared for Wesley several times throughout the story. However, Wesley seemed to forget about Keysha whenever Lori was around. Discuss how Lori was able to keep Wesley so distracted.

6. Maya is trying to establish a strong friendship with Keysha throughout the book. Explain why you feel

Maya is or isn't a good friend. Discuss qualities that a best friend should have.

7. Lori is relentless in her pursuit of Wesley, even though at one point she admits that he's not her type. Why do you think Lori changed her opinion of Wesley?

8. Grandmother Katie comes to Keysha's rescue at her most humiliating moment. Discuss why having someone like Grandmother Katie in Keysha's life is so critical. Does Grandmother Katie remind you of anyone in your family?

9. Keysha reaches a point where she becomes suspicious and fed up with Wesley and his denial of his relationship with Lori. Do you think Keysha was being unreasonable? Why or why not? Also, discuss how you would have felt if you were Keysha and saw your boyfriend kissing another girl.

10. Do you think Keysha jumped into a new relationship with Antonio too soon? Why or why not?

11. Wesley is once again seduced by the false promises of alcohol and begins drinking. Why do you think Wesley decided to go down this road once more? Also, do you know of anyone who has an addiction to alcohol or some other drug? If so, discuss how you're coping with the impact it is having on your life.

12. Dating isn't easy and can sometimes get very complicated with complex issues. If you could give Keysha

and Wesley relationship advice, what would you share with them?

13. Antonio was nothing more than a charming Casanova looking to start intimate relationships with as many girls as possible. However, when he hears the news of Priscilla's pregnancy, he wants nothing more to do with her. Discuss why so many girls like Priscilla get caught up and become teen mothers. Also discuss why boys like Antonio run from their responsibility.

14. How would you go about helping a girlfriend who has learned that she is pregnant? In addition, how would you help a guy who has learned that he has gotten a girl pregnant?

15. Lori was responsible for Wesley getting shot. Do you feel Wesley should've hated her for this? Why or why not?